Who was he, and what was he doing in her cabin?

Now that she'd seen his face, she wasn't as frightened of him, and why was that? There wasn't one cuddly thing about him. She should be running for her life.

Instead, cleaver still in hand, she sat down on a chair opposite him. "You think you fell down a waterfall?" she asked.

"I don't know for sure," he said, touching his lip and wincing.

"You must know *something*," she insisted.

He raised his gaze to hers. "I wish I did, lady, but I'm afraid that what you see is what you get."

ALICE SHARPE

UNDERCOVER MEMORIES

This book is dedicated to my best friend, my lover and my partner—my husband, Arnold Sharpe.

Recycling programs for this product may not exist in your area.

ISBN-13: 978-0-373-74706-1

UNDERCOVER MEMORIES

Copyright © 2012 by Alice Sharpe

www.Harlequin.com

Printed in U.S.A.

ABOUT THE AUTHOR

Alice Sharpe met her husband-to-be on a cold, foggy beach in Northern California. One year later they were married. Their union has survived the rearing of two children, a handful of earthquakes registering over 6.5, numerous cats and a few special dogs, the latest of which is a yellow Lab named Annie Rose. Alice and her husband now live in a small rural town in Oregon, where she devotes the majority of her time to pursuing her second love, writing.

Alice loves to hear from readers. You can write her c/o Harlequin Books, 233 Broadway, Suite 1001, New York, NY 10279. SASE for reply is appreciated.

Books by Alice Sharpe

HARLEQUIN INTRIGUE

746—FOR THE SAKE OF THEIR BABY
823—UNDERCOVER BABIES
923—MY SISTER, MYSELF*
929—DUPLICATE DAUGHTER*
1022—ROYAL HEIR
1051—AVENGING ANGEL
1076—THE LAWMAN'S SECRET SON**
1082—BODYGUARD FATHER**
1124—MULTIPLES MYSTERY
1166—AGENT DADDY
1190—A BABY BETWEEN THEM
1209—THE BABY'S BODYGUARD
1304—WESTIN'S WYOMING‡
1309—WESTIN LEGACY‡
1315—WESTIN FAMILY TIES‡
1385—UNDERCOVER MEMORIES‡‡

*Dead Ringer
**Skye Brother Babies
‡Open Sky Ranch
‡‡The Legacy

CAST OF CHARACTERS

John Cinca—He awakens after apparently falling down a waterfall. He's lost his wallet and his memory. Now he's wanted by both the police and a terrifying killer. If he's going to save his life and that of the woman who risks everything to help him, he needs to find out what happened.

Paige Graham—Left at the altar, she does what any brokenhearted gal would do—she goes on her honeymoon by herself where she can count on the fresh Montana mountain air to rejuvenate her spirit. If she can survive the man she finds in her bed.

Jack Pollock—He's a retired ex-policeman who refuses to even own a gun. That may have been a bad decision on his part.

Anatola Korenev—Big, mean and single-minded, exactly who is this guy and why is he so determined to kill John?

Katy Graham—Paige's little sister's stubborn streak is going to exact a heavy price.

Brian Witherspoon—The man Paige was supposed to marry, he changed his mind at the last moment. However, not everybody knows the wedding didn't take place—some think Paige is his wife, and that means he's in the way....

Natalie Dexter—Clues suggest she is important to John. *How* important is the question.

Chuck Miner—It's generally accepted his coma is due to a beating delivered at the hands of John Cinca. If he can wake up in time, he might be able to reveal the truth.

Matt—A bodybuilder gifted with a streak of nice, he's the one Katy counts on for help. But who's going to help him?

Irina—She knew John many years. What she remembers of his past helps him to not only regain his future, but also catch a glimpse of the man who wants him dead.

Carol Ann Oates—This older woman may hold the key to John's lost memories, and that's why it's imperative he speak with her before it's too late.

Chapter One

Something was wrong.

He must have fallen asleep in a strange position.

He opened his eyes slowly, concentrating for a moment. Rocks, from the size of a pea to a man's fist. Ragged and round, all colors, russet and ivory and gray. A confetti of rocks...

And the nearby thunder of falling water.

But there was something else.

Nausea washed through him as he raised his head, but he kept pushing until he'd dragged himself into a sitting position, wincing as the torn flesh on his hands grated against the rocks. His vision wasn't so good. He gingerly patted his face, felt the puffy skin around his left eye and the tear across his chin. His fingertips came away stained with bright red blood.

He was dressed in a suit, but he was sitting on a rocky beach. The swollen waters of a river washed over his loafer-clad feet, but he was so numb he couldn't feel it. He pulled his legs clear of the water with the same sluggish sense of un-reality with which he took in his surroundings.

Mountains and trees and a rocky riverbank. Rushing water and boulders. The sun was low in the sky. Where was he? How did he get here? He looked upriver and saw the waterfall and then looked down at his torn gray suit and the cuts and bruises on the skin that showed.

Had he fallen down that waterfall?

Who was he? Quick now, what was his name?

Wait. He must have a wallet with identification of some kind.

He patted his soggy suit pockets but found nothing except a few coins. A tight strap across his chest produced a holster under his jacket, and it still cradled a semiautomatic pistol.

What was he doing with a handgun out here of all places? Working on instinct, he pulled back the slide and ejected the clip. He was loaded and ready for—

Ready for what?

He snapped the gun back together and peered down the shoreline. A small bird perched on the tip of a rock. He moved ten feet to the right and targeted a knot on a piece of driftwood. Five seconds later, he pulled the trigger. The wood disintegrated as the startled bird flew toward the trees.

The gun worked.

But the shot echoed along the riverbank, and it came to him with a jolt that he'd just announced his exact location as though issuing a challenge. The hair on the back of his neck stood up; the nearby trees sprouted eyes.

Head spinning, he stumbled to his feet and once again glanced at the sun. It was not only lower in the sky, but drifting behind darkening clouds. He'd been going from one chore to the next at a steady pace, but it must have been in slow motion. There couldn't be more than an hour or two of daylight left, and once the sun went down the temperature would drop. There was already a bluish cast beneath his fingernails, and if he didn't make a point of forbidding it, his teeth clattered together.

But which way did he go?

His gut said he'd come from on top of the bluff. No way he could get back up there before dark. There was no point in following the river and there was no hope of crossing it. He turned toward the forest and started walking. There wasn't a part of him that didn't hurt.

As he limped under the evergreen cover he tripped, falling heavily onto the needled floor. His intention was to get up, keep going. Instead he closed his eyes and sank gratefully into oblivion.

Paige Graham left the Pollocks' cabin soon after dinner, driving off into the rain without looking back.

They were nice people and she'd welcomed their company, even if they were at least a generation her senior. Over the course of the evening she'd learned a lot about them. He was a retired Chicago cop on a pension and she was a retired first-grade teacher. They'd raised four kids and had seven grandchildren. They lived in this area of remote Wyoming mountains year-round, modern-day pioneers who enjoyed a challenge.

In short, they had accomplished what Paige had always dreamed of: a true marriage, a lifetime commitment.

Kind of hard to witness right now. She'd left as soon as it was polite.

She slowed down as the car hit a mud puddle. A moment later, a bolt of lightning flashed in the sky. She counted. One-one-thousand, two-one-thousand... She got to five before thunder shook the car.

It was early in the year to be staying in the mountains, especially for a city girl like her, but she hadn't intended on being here alone. She had six more nights of tranquility ahead of her, but she wasn't sure she could take six more minutes of it.

Some honeymoon.

As she was the only one renting a place during the middle of the week, she wasn't surprised to find the other cabins dark. But her place was unlit, as well, and that did jolt her, as she'd specifically left the porch light burning.

More thunder heralded the dash between the car and the porch. She patted the outside wall, searching for the switch and finding it. It flicked up and down without result, which had to mean the electricity had gone out. The owner had warned this could happen. There was a flashlight inside somewhere. She just wasn't sure where.

Perfect. Now she couldn't even amuse herself watching the one fuzzy channel the antiquated television picked up. She couldn't call anyone because her cell didn't work due to all the trees, nor could she connect to the internet.

And just whom would she communicate with even if she could? Her mother? No, thanks. Her sister? Ditto. Her friends? Man, she'd bet they were having a heyday, half outraged on her behalf, half rabid for details. Who didn't like a nice juicy scandal—besides the people involved in it, of course.

Thoroughly out of sorts now, she unlocked the door and went inside. At least there was a semblance of warmth due to the small fire still burning in the woodstove, and that also gave a tiny bit of light.

A graphic designer by trade, she could probably work on the laptop for a couple of hours. She'd brought along the work for the Red Hook album cover. Surely the battery was up to that, but was she? Maybe it would be best to just go to bed and get the night over with. Tomorrow was a brand-new day, and if it started like this one was ending, she'd drive home early. But if the weather cleared and she was able to stop feeling sorry for herself, she'd take a walk by the river.

She got ready for bed in the dark. The flashlight could wait until morning. As she'd left for this cabin directly from the chapel, the only nightclothes she'd packed had been flimsy little silky wisps appropriate for sashaying in front of a new husband. Needless to say, she hadn't unpacked them. She'd spent the past two nights in sweats and a long-sleeve T-shirt, and they were where she'd left them that morning, hanging over a towel bar in the bathroom, which she found by touch.

She hurried across the freezing floor, contemplating digging in her suitcase for another pair of socks but abandoning that idea because of the dark. She pulled back the covers of the unmade bed and flung herself down onto the mattress, curling into a tight ball and praying for warmth.

And knew immediately she wasn't alone.

Brian...

He'd changed his mind and come after her. She could almost hear him whispering her name.

Did she want him here? No! Who did he think he was?

Funny, she hadn't seen his car.

That wasn't the only thing that was funny. Something smelled kind of earthy.

She reached out a hand slowly and touched a piece of wet fabric. "Brian?" she whispered.

Someone grasped her wrist in a decidedly unfriendly fashion.

Screaming, she wrenched her hand free and bolted out of the bed. But her legs got tangled in the covers and she fell flat on her face. Breathing heavy now, she pulled at the sheet and blankets that constrained her, desperate to escape.

Hands clutched her by the arms and pulled her to her feet. A man—it had to be a man; it was too big to be a woman—shook her.

"Shut up," he said.

Like hell. She screamed louder and kicked.

"Stop it," he said, and shook her again.

She could not get free. Who was this brute who lurked in her bed, wet and steamy and terrifying? What had she been thinking to come to such a remote spot by herself? She could scream all night and no one would hear her.

She gulped a deep breath and tried to gather her thoughts. She had to do something or she'd end up the headline in a newspaper: Woman Found Raped and Beaten to Death in Mountain Cabin.

She shut her mouth and recoiled at the sound of his deep, labored breathing.

"Thank the Lord," he said, and his grip lessened a fraction. She wrenched away again and took off. This time she ran right smack into the wall.

He was there again, towering over her, peeling her away.

"Calm down," he muttered.

"Wouldn't you like that? Who are you? What do you want?"

He was silent. Was he making a list or something? She struggled a little, but his hold on her was firm.

"Turn on the light," he finally said.

"I can't. The electricity is out. Let me go. I'm warning you, my husband will be here any minute and he's ex-military."

His finger rolled over the top of her left hand. "You're not wearing a ring," he said. "And there isn't anything in this cabin to suggest a man was ever here. Don't start yelling again, please. I'm not going to hurt you."

"Who are you?"

It took him a few seconds to mutter, "I don't know."

"What do you mean you don't know?"

"I don't know if I'm Brian," he said, and his voice was strange, too. Slurry, as if he'd been drinking, but his breath didn't smell of booze. "I don't know who I am."

"Will you let go of me if I promise to hear you out?" she asked calmly, but her heart was jumping in her chest. Nothing he said made any sense.

"If you run into the night you'll freeze to death," he warned her.

"If you stand here in those wet clothes much longer, you'll freeze to death, too," she countered.

He slowly dropped his hands.

She scooted out of reach, but this time he didn't come after her. His shape was large in the small room, but a little stooped. His breathing was uneven. "Are you hurt?" she asked.

"Yes."

"How—"

"I don't know."

"So you don't know who you are or how you got hurt."

"No. I may have fallen down a waterfall."

"I'd better have a look at you," she said.

"Are you a doctor?"

"No, but I'm the only other person here, so I guess you have to settle. First I need to find a flashlight. I'm going out to the kitchen."

"Okay," he said, and she heard the squeak of the bedsprings as he sat down.

She took her first deep breath as she left the bedroom, feeling the walls to keep from tripping. The living room wasn't pitch-black, thanks to the meager firelight, but she ran into an ottoman anyway and swore under her breath. She should leave. Damn, her keys were in her jeans pocket, and the pants were back in the bathroom.

Okay, then she should keep going to the door and run back to the Pollocks' house. It was only a mile or so. Better then winding up a headline.

She kept going to the kitchen. She needed that flashlight and maybe a nice big butcher knife.

It took a few minutes of opening drawers and rummaging through the contents in the dark, but her fingers finally touched a smooth, cylindrical object. She fumbled with it until she found a switch and pushed it.

"Let there be light," the man whispered from a few feet away.

She turned the beam onto him. Judging from the arm he threw up to his face, she'd blinded him.

"Sorry," she muttered, lowering the light. She held a cleaver in her right hand, down by her side. If he took one step toward her—

"Well," he said. "Am I?"

"Are you what?"

"Am I Brian?"

Of course he wasn't Brian. His voice was too deep and he was far too big, and anyway, Brian wouldn't act the way this man acted. But she raised the light again to get a good look at her intruder and found a well-built man in his late thirties wearing a torn, wet, bloodstained suit that might once have been pretty sharp looking. His face was scratched and bruised. One eye was puffy and swollen. His bottom lip appeared cut, and there was a split in his chin that probably needed stitches if it wasn't going to leave a scar.

Pushing a mat of thick black hair away from his battered-looking forehead, he gazed at her with dark eyes that revealed nothing. He didn't look like a businessman. In fact, he looked as if he'd be more at home in an alley than in a high-rise, but that could be because he also looked as though he'd gone ten rounds with a prize-fighter—and lost.

"No. You aren't Brian," she said.

"Pity."

She shook her head. "Not really."

He pulled a chair out from the table and sat down as though it was either that or fall on his face.

Who was he, and what was he doing in her cabin? Now that she'd seen his face, she wasn't as frightened of him, and why was that? There wasn't one cuddly thing about him. She should be running for her life.

Instead, cleaver still in hand, she sat down on a chair opposite him, the two of them trapped in a puddle of yellowish light that portended poorly for the flashlight batteries. "You think you fell down a waterfall?" she asked.

"I don't know for sure," he said, touching his lip and wincing.

"You must know *something*," she insisted.

He raised his gaze to hers. "I wish I did, lady, but I'm afraid that what you see is what you get."

Chapter Two

While she built up the fire, he told her about waking up on the riverbank in his current condition. It was a struggle to get the words out. For one thing, his head felt as if it was going to explode. And for another, he was tired beyond endurance.

He didn't mention the gun, which was still in its holster tucked under his jacket. He wasn't sure why he was reluctant to tell her. He just was.

"The second time I woke up I was in the forest. It was almost dark and it was raining," he added as she handed him a cup of tea she'd brewed on the gas stove in the kitchen. She was a restless woman, or maybe she was just nervous, which, given the circumstances, wasn't surprising. Still, given the state of his head, he wished she'd stop moving around so much.

He had a feeling that at any other time in his life, he would have enjoyed watching her move.

She was very slim with blond hair cut kind of uneven in a quirky way, falling long over one side of her face. Her ears were each pierced two times, and she wore small stones that glistened in the flickering light from the fire just as the whites of her eyes did. She looked to be in her late twenties.

"So you just stumbled around until you came to my cabin?" she asked.

"I broke into another one first," he admitted. "But there wasn't anything to eat. Yours looked lived in, so I came through a window in the mudroom. You had food in the fridge and your bed looked too good to pass up." He paused for a heartbeat. "In retrospect, probably not the best idea to pass out in an obviously occupied place, but my thinking was a little fuzzy."

She studied him a minute. "You really don't know your name?"

"No."

"I have to call you something."

"Call me John Doe. It's as good as anything else. What should I call you?"

"Paige Graham. Okay, John Doe. What do you want to do?"

"Sleep," he said, quite honestly. "Though if you want me to leave, I understand."

"I'm not going to force you out into a thunderstorm," she said.

"I appreciate that." He rubbed the back of his neck and did his best not to groan. "How about we put off making further decisions until morning? Maybe if I sleep, my memory will return. You take the bed—"

"That's okay. It's kind of…swampy. You can have it. I'll take the couch. If you'll hand me your damp clothes, I'll hang them here by the fire. And I should bandage a couple of these cuts—"

He waved her off with a limp flick of his fingers. "I'm too tired to worry about anything right now. You're sure about the bed?"

"Positive." He saw the way her gaze flicked toward the front door. There was no way to keep her from leaving as soon as he closed his eyes. Nor was there any way to make sure she didn't use the big knife she'd hidden in the desk drawer unless he tied her up, and he wasn't going to do that. Frankly, at that moment, he didn't particularly care what she did. He had to sleep.

He got to his feet and looked into her gray eyes. "Good night, Paige Graham."

She almost smiled. "Good night, John Doe."

THE LIGHTS WENT ON AT 6:45 a.m. Paige knew this because she'd spent the night sitting on the sofa with the cleaver, just in case. At the moment when the lamp blazed, she was staring at the clock, trying to figure out what to do.

Getting power back made that decision easy. The first order of business was to see if there was anything on the news about an escaped convict or a serial killer. She got up quickly and crossed the room to the small television set that sat inside a hutch. She turned it on and adjusted the old-fashioned rabbit ears until the only channel she'd been able to pick up was clear enough to watch.

She heard the shower start running, but she kept the volume low anyway. More rain was predicted for today. A woman in New York had won the lottery. Firemen had saved a puppy that fell through the grating into a culvert. Interest rates were up. Unemployment was down. She was about to give up and go start a pot of coffee when the picture on the screen changed to one of a forest. A reporter stood next to what appeared to be an abandoned campsite.

As Paige listened to the sketchy details, her fingernails bit into her palms. At a nearby park that was still closed for the season, an unidentified man had been savagely attacked. He'd been airlifted to Green Acre and was listed in critical condition and in a coma. Another man was wanted in connection with the attack. His name was John Cinca and he was a bodyguard working out of Lone Tree, Wyoming. Police were combing the area looking for him. A car rented under his name was found abandoned in the park. Another car was there, as well, abandoned, this one stolen. There were no witnesses and the reason for the attack was unclear.

They flashed a picture of John Cinca on the screen.

John Doe.

Paige found herself standing. She had to get out of here! She ran to the door and looked through the window.

During the night, the rain had turned to snow and left a few inches on the ground. She would leave a visible trail if she attempted to walk away. Her car was *right there*. She had to get her keys.

But John was in the bathroom, and so were her jeans with the keys in the pocket. The bedroom door was ajar and opened the rest of the way noiselessly. She all but floated across the floor to the bathroom. That door opened silently, as well. She could discern the outline of John's body through the shower curtain. Yikes, he was muscular! She grabbed her jeans, closed the door and retraced her steps across the bedroom.

Once in the living room, she pulled the keys from the pocket and snagged her coat and handbag off the back of a chair. She glanced back at the bedroom door—the coast was still clear although the shower had gone off. Man, why hadn't she grabbed her shoes? *No matter, just get out while the getting is good.*

She opened the door and tiptoed onto the deck, avoiding the plank she'd noticed squeaked the day before. Looking back as often as she looked forward, she made it to the car but chose to unlock it with the key rather than risk the noise it made with the keyless entry button. The door opened quietly and she slipped inside. She left the door unlatched but the car started beeping when she inserted the key, so she closed it, wincing at the thud it made.

Taking a deep breath, she turned the key while staring at the front door. The car roared to life, but at that second, the door opened and John emerged wearing his slacks and nothing else, glaring at her as he advanced across the porch.

"Stop," he yelled.

Sure. Pushing down on the gas pedal, she jammed the shift into Reverse. The car jerked backward. John looked mad enough to jump in front of the car. Let him.

Instead, he raised his hand and she saw what she hadn't noticed before. He was holding a gun.

Merciful heavens. He was going to kill her!

She shifted into forward and gunned the engine again, but the back end had apparently wound up in a ditch or something and the car wouldn't go forward. The tires just spun uselessly in the muddy snow.

She reached down and pushed the door lock button, still revving the engine and going nowhere fast.

He was at her window. "Stop the car," he demanded.

The rearview mirror revealed blue smoke billowing out the tailpipe. There was no point in burning up her engine. She took her foot off the gas pedal.

"Stop the car and get out," he said. He didn't raise the gun; he didn't need to. He knew he'd won.

She switched off the engine and pounded on the steering wheel, then opened the car door.

He grabbed her arm and hauled her out. His powerful chest was as bruised and battered as his arms. "Get in the house," he said.

She walked through the snow, her feet in the wet socks freezing now. He was barefoot and gave no sign he even felt it.

"This is the thanks I get for letting you have the bed?" she snarled as he closed the front door behind them.

"You mean the swamp?" He ran a hand through

his hair. "What happened, Paige? Why did you bolt?"

So, what did she do? Inform him he was wanted for nearly killing a man? Might that not give him ideas? Her gaze strayed to the television. She hadn't turned it off but the volume was so low she couldn't hear it from ten feet away. The same reporter as before was back on the screen. They were replaying the same story.

She looked away, but too late. She'd caught John's attention, and he stepped behind her to see what she had been watching. His picture filled the screen, then faded away as an ad came on.

John looked down at her, the gun by his side.

"Why was my picture on television?"

"You seriously beat a man," she said. There was no point in not telling him. All he had to do was wait for the story to loop around again.

"Tell me what you know."

She repeated the few details, pausing after announcing he was actually John Cinca, looking for some sign the name clicked with him. There wasn't one. He made a brief comment about the coincidence of giving himself a pseudonym that was actually his real first name, but that was it.

Next she told him he was a bodyguard living

in a city two hundred miles away and that he'd rented a car that was still in the campground although probably impounded by now.

As she spoke, he made a fist of his left hand and gazed at his knuckles as though searching for proof he couldn't have beaten someone senseless. But his hands were not only large and powerful, they were covered with bruises and cuts. And the knots of muscles in his chest and upper arms that flexed when he moved were further proof that if motivated, he could easily inflict some serious harm.

A shiver of fear snaked down Paige's spine. There wasn't an ounce of fat on his lean frame. Whoever he was, he kept himself fit.

"So, you tried to leave because you realized you were in a small cabin with a would-be killer," he said.

"What would you have done?" she whispered.

"Tried to leave." He shook his head. "I obviously have a gun. Why would I beat someone up?"

"I don't know, John. Noise, maybe?"

"Where did this happen?"

"At the park on top of the bluff."

"I wonder how I ended up in the river. Wait, were there eyewitnesses?"

"They didn't mention any."

"Then they don't know for sure I did it, right?"

"I don't think so. But they're looking for you. It's only a matter of time before they start checking out these cabins, you know."

He nodded in a distracted fashion.

"What are you going to do?" she asked him.

"Beats me."

"Well, for starters, could you maybe put the gun away?"

He fiddled with it for a second, she assumed flicking on the safety. Then he looked into Paige's eyes and offered her the gun.

"What are you doing?"

"You have to look out for yourself. If I'm capable of something like what you described—"

"Then you could easily kill me with your bare hands," she said, and then stepped back inside her mind and stared at herself a second. Was she crazy? The man had confronted her over the barrel of a gun just a few minutes ago. She took the weapon. It was the first time in her life she'd ever held a gun, and she was surprised at how heavy it was.

She handed it back to him. "Take out the bullets."

He ejected what looked like a slender package of cigarettes. "It's called a clip."

"Give me the clip, then, and you keep the gun."

He smiled at her.

Okay, really, he had the sexy, glowering alpha male bit down to a T. In fact it seemed effortless. But when he smiled, he turned into a guy who probably had a perfectly normal life somewhere. A wife maybe, or a girlfriend. Children. A mortgage.

Again, she took a mental step back. Had she just dismissed the fact that he had probably beaten a man to a pulp less than twenty-four hours before? No, but it was hard to believe it was true. Impossible, almost. He could just as easily have been another victim, or the injured man might have attacked him first.

"Would you really have shot me?" she asked.

"No," he admitted. "I just grabbed the gun like it was a habit of some kind."

"There's a first-aid kit in the kitchen. A couple of your wounds need bandaging. I'll get it for you." When she returned with the kit, he thanked her.

"We both could use some coffee and food, and then I think we better get you to the police," she said as she took off the coat and hooked it over the back of a chair.

He'd looked cooperative until the last part. He shook his head. "No way."

"I'm putting on a pot of coffee. We'll talk about it."

"You can talk all you want," he said. "I'm going to finish getting dressed."

"Aren't you afraid I'll take off as soon as you close the bedroom door?"

Now he laughed, and if the smile had transformed him, the laughter lit him from the inside, even as he flinched and touched his lip. "After the way you jammed your car into that ditch? Not really."

He turned to walk back to the bedroom, and that's when she saw the scars on his back. Paige produced an involuntary gasp.

"What's wrong?" he asked, whirling to face her.

She approached him. "You've been burned in the past. Your back is scarred." She resisted the urge to touch him, the first such urge she'd had. All this bare, male flesh reminded her she was supposed to be here with her new husband....

"So are my legs," he said. "And there's a three-inch scar on my thigh. I think I've led a colorful life."

"That's one way to put it," she said.

He turned away and then back again. "If you do think of a way to get out of here in the next few minutes, will you do me a favor?"

"I don't know. What do you want?"

"Don't turn me over to the cops, okay?"

"I'll think about it," she said, but the truth was she wasn't going anywhere. And she had the feeling he knew that damn well.

Chapter Three

There was no option but to redress in the torn clothes he'd woken up in. They were still on the damp side and were getting pretty ripe. He slapped a bandage on his chin and one on his forehead and called it good.

Man, he was a mess. The eye wasn't as puffy as before, but he had at least a day's growth of dark beard to go with the bruises and cuts. No wonder Paige had looked frightened of him—he was the bogeyman of a nightmare.

"You sorry bastard," he told his reflection.

There was something else, too. He'd had dreams during the night. Vivid ones. They'd woken him in a cold sweat, driven him into the shower to try to wash away the images. Faces of children, fire, mayhem. Screams...

Like a war. And something flying, hovering, threatening.

Was he a soldier or had he been one in his youth? And what about the children in the dream? Had he done something terrible to children? He couldn't believe that of himself. He didn't know *who* he was, but he did have a sense of *what* he was, and it wasn't a murderer.

Yet even now, wide awake, remembering the images made his stomach roll like a set of slow ocean waves.

He splashed cold water on his face and told himself to get a grip. His memory would return any minute and he'd figure out what went wrong, what had happened to him, and maybe more important, what he'd done to someone else.

The aroma of coffee drew him into the kitchen, where Paige handed him a mug, then set a plate of scrambled eggs in front of him.

"What is it like? I mean, not knowing who you are?" she asked as she sat opposite him again.

"Weird," he said as the first hot swallow of coffee washed down his throat. "Empty."

"About the police—"

He'd picked up his fork but set it aside again. "No police. Not until I can remember what happened. I'm willing to face the music when it comes to paying for my crimes, but if they've decided I've almost killed a man, how can I prove I didn't?"

"Then how about getting some expert help?"

"Like a shrink?"

"No, like a retired cop. I happened to have had dinner with one last night. He and his wife seem like real down-to-earth types. He might be able to advise you about what to do next."

He picked up the fork again and took a few bites. The eggs tasted pretty good. They were the first thing he'd eaten since stealing yogurt out of Paige's refrigerator the evening before.

He studied her for a minute. "Who's Brian?"

She looked away from him.

"You called me that last night."

"I remember."

"So, who is he?"

"Brian Witherspoon. He *was* my fiancé up until about three days ago."

"Who broke up with who?"

"And that is your business because?"

"Because my head is a vast wasteland. Give me something to think about besides my life, which currently sucks big-time. Throw me a bone. Have a heart. Anyway, I'm curious. You got tired of him, right?"

"You think so?"

"Yes. Hard to picture someone skipping out on you, so you must have done the skipping. Then you came up here by yourself to get away from his incessant pleas to get back together. How am I doing?"

"Perfectly," she said. Then she blinked, her

eyes bright, and shook her head. "Actually, he left me. At the altar. In front of everyone when his ex-wife showed up for the wedding. The preacher said that line about anyone having doubts, and she stood up and announced she still loved him."

"Ouch."

"So I came on my honeymoon by myself. Pathetic, huh?"

"I think it's kind of gutsy."

"How about you show some guts? Come with me to talk to Jack Pollock. He's a good man."

"He's a cop."

"Ex-cop."

"Same thing."

"Well, there now, see? You know something about yourself after all. You don't like the police."

He finished off his eggs. "I also know cops are all alike."

"That's silly. Of course they aren't. Anyway, I told you, he's retired."

"He's still a gun-toting—"

"No, as a matter of fact, you're wrong. His wife told me last night that he won't have a gun in the house. He's left all that behind him. And as for gun toting, that seems to describe you, doesn't it?"

He stared at her a second and sighed. "Yeah,

I guess so. Okay, you win, we'll go see your friend."

"Good. I'll clean up and get dressed while you figure out how to get my car out of the ditch."

He watched her turn to the sink. She was wearing a tight pair of jeans that made her rear look pretty damn enticing. She turned back, leaning down to take his plate, and their gazes locked. She wasn't wearing a bra, which was evident every time she moved. The look in her eyes gave him the impression she knew exactly what he was thinking.

His gaze landed on something gold and silver and shiny hanging from a chain around her neck. It had slipped out from beneath her clothes when she leaned forward and now lay against her blue T-shirt between her breasts.

He sucked in his breath and didn't know why.

"What is it?" she asked, her voice alarmed.

"Your necklace—"

"This?" She fingered the pendant. "Is something wrong with it?" she added as she lowered her gaze to look.

He shook his head, embarrassed by his visceral, gut-level reaction to such a silly thing.

"My father gave it to me," she said. "It's an owl, see? His little wings move up and down and his eyes are tiny topazes—"

She stopped talking, her expression alarmed. "You look spooked, John. Why?"

He shook his head. "I don't know. That thing just creeps me out."

She slipped the owl under her shirt again. "All better?"

"Yeah," he said, but even knowing it was there made him antsy. He pushed the chair away from the table. "I'll see about the car," he said, anxious to move around a little and get his feelings under control.

It took a shovel, three old boards and a little digging, but he freed the car just as Paige emerged from the cabin. She'd changed clothes and donned a coat. Beneath its unbuttoned contours, he could see the thin strap of her purse bisecting her torso. Looked as if she'd put a bra on under a blue sweater, which was a shame, but at least the damn pendant was covered.

With her bright eyes and fresh face, she looked like a coed on her way to a class—way too young for him, not just in years but in life experience.

Which was an odd thing to think, as he couldn't recall any life experiences before about eighteen hours before, but he still knew it was true. The gun that felt so natural in his hand was a good indicator of that. He got into the passenger seat and she slid behind the wheel.

"How far away are these people?" he asked.

"About a mile. In fact, they're closer to the river than I am. I'm surprised you didn't stumble on them first. I can't call ahead because my cell doesn't work up in these mountains."

"Maybe they won't be home," he said hopefully.

But a few minutes later they found a brand-new truck parked on a quiet wooded street in front of a modest green cabin. The few other houses around it looked empty.

Okay, one way or another he was going to have to trust a complete stranger, which come to think of it, pretty much described the entire population of the world except for Paige Graham. He sure hoped this didn't turn out to be the mother of stupid ideas.

He followed Paige up the front steps, where she knocked on the door and rang the bell.

"Maybe they're still asleep," he said as they stood on their side of the unanswered door.

Paige tried the knob. The door opened as far as the dead bolt chain allowed. She called out, "Jack? Carolyn?"

There was no answer.

"Maybe they went for a walk," Paige said. "That's where I met them, on a morning hike in the forest."

"Well, what a shame we missed them," he said.

She started to close the door, then stopped. "No, they're not out hiking. I can see Jack's backpack over there on the floor. He told me he always takes it with him because he likes to be prepared."

"A cop *and* a Boy Scout. Great." He pointed at the steps. "There are no tracks in the snow except ours."

"Maybe they're around back."

"In this weather?"

"Don't give up so easily," she said, and marched down the steps and around the house like a general off to mount an attack. Once again he followed.

But the back of the house was as empty as the front. Paige sighed and said, "Well, we struck out, I guess. I could leave a note, maybe, or something."

He caught her hand and pointed at the back door. It was closed, but what had caught his attention were the tracks that crossed the small deck toward a smaller door that probably opened into a garage.

Paige tore her hand out of his and ran up the stairs to the deck. He called her name, begged her to stop, but she was inside the house in a flash and once again he followed.

He arrived in the kitchen to find more prints on the floor and Paige disappearing down the hall. The smell of death lay heavy in the heated house.

Paige turned into a room on the right, and then she screamed. The sound sent chills down John's back as he raced to help her. Still screaming, she backed out of the room, hands held in front as though warding away evil, her gaze riveted on whatever lay within.

John grabbed her shoulders. She turned into his chest and buried her face against him, the screams morphing into sobs, her body shaking violently. He peered over her head.

An older woman lay in the bed as though she'd been killed in her sleep, her throat slit. Blood sprayed the wall behind her, soaked into her bedding, pooled on the floor.

"Where's Jack?" Paige mumbled as John pulled her from the doorway.

Good question. Still holding on to each other, they searched the small house but found no sign of the old guy. "We have to get out of here," John told her at last.

She seemed too stunned to argue. He hurried her back the way they had come. Once out the door, he stopped abruptly. The footprints leading to the garage now took on an ominous feel. John opened the door with the fabric of his jacket, hoping against hope he wasn't about to find what he knew in his gut he would.

"Stay back a minute," he said, but Paige had already peered around him and they both saw Jack Pollock at the same time.

He was in his pajamas and slippers, and it appeared he'd been attacked by a maniac with a hatchet. There was so much blood it was hard to see what the man had once looked like. The car was gone, leaving tire tracks of red against the cement.

Paige was unnaturally silent and John looked down at her with concern. Her mouth was open, her eyes shut, as though she was lost in a cacophony of silent screams that ricocheted inside her head.

He pulled on her once again. "Come with me," he said, closing the door behind them. They quickly retraced their path in the snow, both of them looking around as they moved for some sign they weren't alone. This time John shuffled his feet, obliterating any of their clear footprints.

"Someone murdered them and stole their car," Paige mumbled.

"Yes."

"I should have called the police from their phone," she said as they reached the car. Without discussing it, she handed John the keys.

"They're way past needing immediate attention," he said, opening her door for her.

"But we can't just leave them—"

"Yes, we can," he said gently.

He closed her door and went around to his own side, slipping behind the wheel.

"John, you know what this means, don't you?" she asked.

"I probably didn't hurt the guy up at the park, yeah, I know."

"Someone else—"

"Some kind of maniac," he interrupted.

"Yes. I want to leave the mountains. Now."

"Right now?"

"As soon as I get my computer. I can't leave that behind. All my work is on it. You can come with me if you want, but I can't stay here. Not after...not after this."

His gut twisted as he stared at her swollen eyes and pale face. In some illogical way, he knew he was responsible for what was going on. He could feel it in his bones.

"Let's just hurry," he said at last. "I don't think those murders happened all that long ago." He paused to look down the street and back the way they'd come. He saw no movement that suggested the killer hovered nearby, but threat seemed to hang in the air like cold, damp fog.

"I'll be quick," she said, her voice shaky. Tears ran down her cheeks and she flicked them away with her fingertips. He fought the urge to comfort her by starting the car. He didn't dare touch her. He wanted it far too much and he wasn't sure why, but the feeling their fates were interconnected had grown strong in the past few hours and the thought that whoever had done that to the Pollocks could do the same to Paige was more awful than he could bear contemplating.

"I'll leave the mountains with you," he told her. "For better or worse, we're in this together."

She covered her face with her hands.

He let her cry in peace.

BACK AT THE CABIN, PAIGE dumped her coat on the bed and threw her belongings into her bag. She and John split up the rest of the chores, with John hauling things out to her car. She worked fast, although a combination of nerves and the vivid images of the Pollocks' bloodied bodies made her clumsy.

John was outside packing the trunk when she took a last check of the kitchen. Might as well take things to eat on the road. As she grabbed a few apples and a chunk of cheese, she heard the back door open.

"John?" Closing the fridge door, she turned, intending to ask him to help her carry the last load out to the car.

It wasn't John.

The cheese slid from her grasp and hit the wood floor at her feet with a clunk.

"Who are you?" she gasped, but she already knew.

The man filling the doorway six feet away had shaggy black hair streaked with white, and small, mean eyes. Though he wasn't as tall as John, he was built like a bull, with strong-looking shoulders and big hands with a band of black and gold on the right ring finger. His face was etched with deep lines, his lips thick and curled in a sneer. The bulky jacket with a fur collar that he wore stretched tight across his chest and pulled at the one button he'd managed to secure.

Paige's stomach flipped as she recognized the coat. It had belonged to Jack Pollock. Thin, wiry Jack Pollock. That's why the coat was too tight for this man. The revulsion she felt was nothing compared with the horror that filled her as the light from the one weak bulb hanging from the ceiling glanced off the thick, curved blade of a dagger he held down by his leg....

This was the man who had attacked and killed the Pollocks—she knew that as surely as she knew anything, and would have even if their blood hadn't stained his shoes, even if he didn't carry that knife or wear that jacket. She could see it in his eyes. She could smell it. He was a predator and he was ruthless.

And from the look on his face, she was his next victim.

Terror momentarily drained her, anchoring her to the floor. And then just as quickly, the instinct to flee melted indecision.

She threw the apples at his face, turned and ran.

Out of the corner of her eyes she saw him react way faster than she'd expected. She screamed John's name as she raced into the living room. The door seemed a mile away. She screamed again. Where was John? Had this beast already killed him?

The man's heavy footsteps pounded right behind hers. He caught her hair and pulled her back against him right as the door flew open and John appeared.

Their gazes locked.

He held his gun, but he had to know, as did she, that it was empty.

What good was an unloaded gun against a monster?

Chapter Four

"Mr. Cinca," the man said in a thickly accented voice that sounded as if it came from inside a fish tank.

John winced. How did this guy know his name? "Who are you?" he asked.

"Come now. Don't play coy with me." He smiled—if you could call it that—and added, "You look surprised to see me again. You thought you got away. But what is a waterfall to man like me? I walk down long way when I hear shot, but I arrive in one piece. Now put down gun. The chase is over. No more games. Anatola Korenev has won."

The guy's accent nudged itself against the void of John's missing memory. For the first time since waking up on the riverbank, he felt close to grabbing on to something about himself, but the feeling had no sooner blossomed than it wilted away.

"How did you know I was here in *this* cabin?"

John asked, biding for time. He had to figure out where Paige had put the ammo clip. He should have collected it the minute they got back here. What was wrong with him?

"I followed you from old people's house. Good luck for me I see you. You are losing your touch. Maybe rocks bang you on head too hard."

"Maybe," John said, swearing silently at himself. He'd known better than to agree to come back here, but he'd been so moved by Paige's grief he'd allowed sentiment to get in the way of survival. And now it looked as though they were both going to pay for it.

He'd been trying hard not to meet Paige's gaze, afraid he'd weaken if he saw her fear. When he finally did, he found anger burning behind the terror. And then she glanced at the desk drawer and back at him. She'd stuck the giant knife there the night before—had she put the ammo there this time?

"I propose a trade," Korenev said.

"What kind of trade?" John asked as he gauged the distance he had to cover to get to the drawer.

"Hand over gun and girl goes free."

"Oh, come on," John said. "Did you try the same lame thing on the Pollocks before you murdered them?"

"Not exactly," Korenev said.

"I don't get it," John said. "Why did you kill them that way?"

Korenev shrugged. "Old man caught me stealing car. Had to die. Woman might hear car start and look out window. Anyway," he added, shrugging, "overkill suggests crazy person. Someone like you, maybe. Give me gun or girl will be dead before she hits floor."

"Go to hell," Paige managed to gasp. It earned her another throat-tightening squeeze, and this time John saw the gold on the man's finger. Paige's body grew limp and her eyes rolled back.

"Here," John said, holding the gun by the barrel with the empty grip down and pointed away from the brute's sight. He advanced a few steps and didn't have to work to inject panic in his voice. "Leave her alone, take the gun, let her go, I'll come with you."

"Put the gun down," Korenev repeated.

But John kept advancing, talking a mile a minute as though he couldn't stop himself. "No, no, you take it, here, please, just take it, let her go, don't hurt her, I'll come with you, let her go...."

He was finally close enough to shove the revolver at the guy, who grabbed it by the grip. John steeled himself to take whatever opportunity presented itself.

Paige, more or less cast aside in the transaction, slumped to the floor. A second later, it was obvious Korenev realized the ammo clip was missing. Enraged, he threw the gun at John, who dodged to the left. The weapon landed beside him and slid across the floor out of sight into the bedroom.

The attacker came at him with the knife held above his head, roaring like a banshee.

Paige was a blur at the desk as John fought to avoid the blade directed at his chest. "The clip is in my coat!" she yelled. John avoided the downward slash of the knife. Paige's coat was on the bed. At least he thought it was. Six short feet to save the day. Might as well be six hundred....

Barely dodging another slice-and-dice attempt, he glimpsed Paige advancing with the cleaver in her hand. Their attacker must have sensed her behind him. He turned quickly and slashed at her as she raised the cleaver to protect her head.

Suddenly, the room filled with screams of pain and a geyser of spurting blood. For one terrible moment, John thought Korenev had slit Paige's throat. But it wasn't she who was injured. With the force of his own strength, Korenev had driven his right hand across the cleaver blade and lost his index finger in the process. His bellows rattled the windows as he tucked his maimed, bloody hand under his arm and advanced on Paige with a murderous fire burning in his eyes.

Paige had dropped the cleaver in the impact and was now backed against the wall as John darted into the bedroom to get the ammo. Her coat was on the bed but it had four pockets, all zipped, and he wasted precious time feeling around trying to find the right one as Paige's screams pealed through the cabin. At the same time, he scanned the floor, in search of the gun. There it was, against a floorboard on the outside wall. He finally found the right pocket.

He soon slid the clip into the grip and lunged back into the living area. Paige and the killer were gone. He heard an engine start out back and ran through the kitchen in time to spot a gold car emerge from behind a copse of evergreen trees, Paige behind the wheel.

John fired off a couple of shots at the tires, but he was too late. It was too far away.

Swearing, he raced back into the house.

"Drive fast," Korenev demanded. With his good hand, he held the knife tip against Paige's throat.

"I said fast," Korenev repeated, and leaning toward her, stomped his boot on top of her right foot, depressing the accelerator even farther, ignoring her cries of pain as he crushed her toes. Shoved against the driver's door, she could barely breathe and the trees flying by her window made her head spin.

As they came to a crossroad, he grabbed the wheel with his bloody hand, swinging it hard to the right. The car turned widely, hitting a ditch but bouncing back onto the pavement, careening across both lanes as Korenev fought to regain control. Paige held her breath as the smell of his fresh blood combined with terror made her stomach heave.

With the crazy turn, they'd left the main highway that would have taken them out of the mountains. If John was following, he would undoubtedly continue on straight.

If John was following.

What had Korenev meant when he claimed he'd butchered the Pollocks to make it appear the work of a madman, a man like John? Was John a cold-blooded killer?

As if it mattered right now? If she had to choose her poison, John or this guy, bring on John. *Please...*

Korenev was breathing kind of shallow. He'd lost a lot of blood. She had to keep focused. If the man blacked out, it would be up to her to get the car stopped without crashing it.

Think, think, think. You still have your purse.

What's in it that you can use? Why didn't you buy a spray can of pepper spray when you had the chance? Or a little gun?

With a sinking heart, the only object she was sure she carried besides a wallet were her car keys.

It became obvious that Korenev had no intention of giving in to pain or injury when he finally took some of his weight off her foot. His big hand still clamped the steering wheel over hers.

They were approaching a wide spot in the road. On one side was a closed-up gas station and on the other a small square building, a tavern called Gil's Place.

Korenev turned the car into a parking area beside the tavern that appeared to be carved out of the surrounding dense forest. There was a sprinkling of other vehicles, but not many; after all, it was not yet noon. He made straight for the back of the lot, easing up on the pedal and searching for something.

When he seemed to find what he wanted, he finally shifted his bulk back into his own seat and took his hand off the wheel, his foot off of hers. The relief lasted about one second.

"Drive in forest over there," he said, gesturing with the knife. "Hurry."

He'd chosen an area where the underbrush

wasn't as heavy. There was the suggestion of a track, perhaps a leftover from a logging road years before.

She hesitated. Who knew what horror he had in mind for her, and surely the middle of the lot was a better place to face her fate than the deep cover of the trees?

The knife tip grazed her skin. "Do it," he said.

She drove into the forest, following his directions, tears stinging her eyes because she was so scared and because she couldn't find even the smallest sliver of hope.

Stop it, she admonished herself. *There's always hope.*

"That's far enough," he said. As the car had more or less burrowed as deep into the forest as possible without the aid of a bulldozer, she eased off the gas and turned off the car.

"Give me your purse," he said.

She took it from around her body and handed it to him. Her hands were surprisingly steady.

"Open it."

She unzipped the bag and he peeked inside. "Put it on dashboard," he directed, apparently satisfied she wasn't carrying a weapon around in her bag.

Again she did as he said.

Staring right into her eyes, knife held firmly in his bloody maimed hand, Korenev unbuckled his belt and started tugging it through the belt loops.

Surely he wasn't thinking rape!

But what about the way he'd staged the Pollocks' murders? Bile rose up her throat. Who knew what this man would do? The door on her side was wedged against a tree or she would have taken her chances. As it was, she was trapped.

He pulled the belt loose and quickly tugged the free end back through the buckle, then slipped it over Paige's head, sliding it down until it circled her neck. The buckle bit against her flesh, yanked on her hair. In essence, he'd created a collar for her and he controlled the "leash."

"One good tug and eyes pop," he said in such a matter-of-fact way her blood turned to water.

"Yes, okay."

"Who are you? How you know Cinca?"

"I don't. I'm just renting the cabin."

"Give me wallet. Hurry. I'm late."

Late for what? Murder, mayhem? She took out the blue wallet, a gift from Brian. She'd forgotten that until this moment.

"Show me driver's license."

She did. He studied it for a second. "Paige Graham," he said. "So, you are nobody, huh? Tell the truth. How you know Cinca?"

It was on the tip of her tongue to repeat that she didn't know John, he'd just arrived much like Korenev himself, but then she thought better of it. If Korenev didn't believe John would come after her, what use was she to Korenev?

"We're lovers," she said.

He raised his thick eyebrows and sneered. "Oh, come now. You expect I believe that?"

"I don't care what you believe. It's a fact. John and I are lovers."

"There was no sign of you at his place in Lone Tree."

She shrugged. "We, um, conducted our affair at my place."

"Why?"

"I was involved with someone else. So what?"

He narrowed his eyes as he seemed to really look at her for the first time. There was speculation in his black eyes, and doubt.

"Why else would he risk his life for me?" she added.

"So he arrange to meet you here after…business?"

This was thin ice, although the thought that John had had "business" with this man appalled her. Nevertheless, she'd started this, and she knew she had to keep it simple or get tripped up in her own lies. He obviously didn't realize John didn't remember anything past yesterday, and he just as clearly wasn't a close friend. She nodded.

He produced a leer that literally made her skin crawl. She'd heard the expression, of course, but this was the first time she'd experienced it, and it was creepy.

He tossed her purse and wallet on the floor, then pulled up his trouser leg, revealing a holster into which he slid the knife. Paige took a shaky breath. He could still choke her, but at least it wasn't likely he'd slit her throat.

For now, anyway.

He caught the handle on the passenger-side door and heaved his bulk against it, keeping the belt tight around Paige's throat as he bullied the door open. The buckle pressed into her flesh. Somehow he managed to extricate himself from the car, tugging her along behind him, yanking on her arm when she didn't move fast enough for him. Then he shoved her ahead of him until they cleared the car.

"Walk fast. One word and you die," he said.

It was on the tip of her tongue to say, "Yeah, yeah, you said that already," and then she wondered again if she'd lost her senses.

As soon as they cleared the trees, she looked back, positive there would be an obvious path to the gold car, but it was as though the forest had closed in around the recent wound. She scanned the parking lot instead. Surely there would be someone around to witness this bizarre kidnapping, someone to either call for help or whip out a big old six-shooter.

No one. Not a soul. Just a half dozen cars and a squat one-story building rising from the melting snow with no discernible windows. The faint melody of a country-western song was the only sound besides the crunching of their feet on the quickly thawing ground.

He paused long enough to take the knife out again and thrust it toward her to show he meant business. How crazy was this—that a man could march a woman through a parking lot in broad daylight with a belt around her neck and a knife at her back and no one saw it?

Using the bulk of his body and the threat of the knifepoint, Korenev finally pushed Paige against the side of an old car parked deep in the shadows amid a couple of other clunkers. He reached around her and shattered the passenger window with his closed fist. "Open it," he said.

Avoiding the glass, she pulled up the lock and opened the door. The bench front seat was much torn and patched with duct tape, though here and there a spring managed to poke through. The steering wheel was wrapped in tape, as well, and the dashboard fairly gleamed silver with the stuff.

"Empty it," he ordered, using the knife to point to the glove box, which was missing its cover. Most of the contents had already spilled to the floor mat below. She pulled out a partial roll of the same tape that seemed to hold the interior of the car together and a few odds and ends, revealing at last a small yellow button.

"That's it," he said, his satisfied breath hot against the back of her neck. "Push it."

A twanging sound announced the trunk had popped open. "My lucky day," he added as he picked up the duct tape.

With a sinking feeling for what was coming next, she thought of and discarded scenarios as fast as she could. Kicking him, clawing him, screaming at the top of her lungs, grabbing at his injured hand—

But each idea came overlaid with the image of Jack Pollock's brutal death, to say nothing of the knowledge that Korenev would happily use his muscles to either tighten the belt around her neck or plunge the knife into her chest.

He ordered her to go around to the back of the car. "Tape you ankles," he demanded.

"But—"

With a sudden yank of the belt, he leaned in close to her face. "Understand," he said softly. "You are little value to me. I keep you alive just to use as bait to trap Cinca. Now tape ankles together on skin and do it tight or I will cut my losses—and your throat."

As he had Carolyn Pollock's...

Leaning over, she wound the tape around her legs. When she straightened up, he grabbed the tape from her hand and bit off a piece. As he pushed it toward her mouth, she turned her head. Closing his fist, he fought her resistance with a punch on the cheekbone that all but knocked her out. She sagged, but he caught her, and ripping off a new piece, slapped it over her mouth. "Be grateful I not cover your nose, too," he growled as he bound her wrists in back of her, using just the one hand and yet working so fast and with such ease that it was as though he'd done it that way his whole life.

The next thing she knew, he'd lifted her off her feet and dumped her into the trunk. She landed on something hard and cold, a rod or a pipe. The lid made a deafening sound as it slammed shut over her head.

Lying alone in the cold, black enclosure, she waited for the car to start.

A few minutes later, the engine made a few putting noises. He must have tried to hot-wire it. Bracing herself for the worst, Paige waited for whatever came next.

Chapter Five

John ran back into the kitchen, skidding when his foot landed on an apple. He kicked it out of the way and continued on into the living room, where momentum temporarily deserted him.

Paige was gone, stolen away. The cabin was suddenly as empty as John's head.

Where were her car keys? He'd driven them back from the Pollocks' house. He hit his own pockets a half dozen times, his thoughts all jumbled and confused. They'd come home from the Pollocks' house desperate to get out of the mountains. He'd popped the trunk with the electronic button and then he'd—he'd handed the damn keys to Paige, that's what he'd done, and she'd opened the cabin door. She must have the keys.

Or they were in her coat or her purse.

That purse had been strapped across her body. Her coat was in the bedroom....

The weird thing on the floor he was staring

at finally resolved itself into Anatola Korenev's bloody, severed digit. John hurried back into the kitchen and found a plastic bag in a drawer. He picked up the finger with the bag and deposited it in the freezer, marking it with an ink pen: *police evidence*. Maybe someday the prints lifted from that finger would come in handy—who knew?

He had to find those keys. The coat turned up nothing, and there just wasn't anyplace else to look. Grabbing the jacket, he rushed out to the car and threw it in the backseat. She'd need it when he found her—if he found her.

Then he started an outward search of the vehicle.

As he investigated with his hands all the usual places to hide a key, he considered using the on-board satellite service he'd noticed mounted in the car during their drive to the Pollocks' house. He was pretty sure if he pushed the right button, the company could start it remotely, but really, would they do that without a password or something? Highly improbable. More likely they'd notify the cops, and boy, he really did not want that.

Did he have that right, though? Paige's life was in danger because she'd been kind to him; he should call the cops and think about her safety and not his own. And yet in the back of his fuzzy brain he was certain that Paige's best chance for survival was John himself. Korenev had gone to great ends to find him, and he must have taken Paige in the hope he could use her. As soon as he figured out he couldn't, who knew what he'd do?

A minute later, while running his fingers up under the right rear wheel well, John felt the metallic hide-a-key box and damn near yelled with relief. He wasn't sure how much of a head start they had; somehow he'd lost track of time again, but he drove as fast as he dared on the snowy road. With so little traffic, the tracks were easy to see, and he took a breath of relief. This would be easier than he'd thought it would be. All he had to do was follow the—

No, it wasn't going to be that easy, because a couple of miles down the road, the snow had all but melted on the tarmac and by the time he came to a four-corner crossroad, it was impossible to tell which way Korenev and Paige had gone. There was nothing to indicate one road was better than another except a sign announcing the main highway up ahead. That sounded promising. He went straight.

Traffic picked up and he began to wonder how this situation would ever be resolved. It seemed there were dozens of gold or tan cars like the Pollocks' on the road.

As he drove, he racked his brain for some memory of Korenev or the waterfall. The man had made some pretty nasty statements.... What was going on? Did he and Korenev know one another? Heaven forbid, were they partners? Oh, please, not that.

One thing was obvious—Korenev was unaware John had lost his memory. Maybe there would be a way to work that to his own advantage.

He'd just driven up a rise when the sight in the small valley below caused him to pull over to the side of the road. The police had set up a roadblock, and a growing line of cars waited to be cleared.

No way Korenev would chance that if he had any other option. No way John could chance it, either. He didn't have a driver's license, he looked as if he'd been attacked by a bear and he was driving a car registered to someone else.

He turned around and went back the way he'd come.

When he got to the four corners, he pulled over again and walked the intersection, crossing each street and bending to look closely at the ground, searching for some sign that they'd come this way. There were no buildings and no one around to point a finger and say, "They went that way."

The only thing he saw out of place were parallel tracks two tires had made in the verge. It looked fresh to him. But this was the smallest and least-traveled-looking of the roads, and his instincts said to try the others first.

Thirty minutes later, after a dead end and a road that looped around to connect to the main highway, he set off down the smaller road. Had he ever had good instincts? Were they messed up now due to the fall and amnesia, or was he always a screwup?

It wasn't long before he came across a closed-up gas station on one side of the road and a run-down-looking tavern on the other. There were two old guys in the parking lot and a few vehicles, but other than that it was dead.

There was something about the two old men, though, that set off a warning bell. The way they stood in the center of the lot was odd, for one thing, as were their confused expressions. He pulled into the lot and got out of the car, attempting to look respectable despite his shredded suit and the bruises and Band-Aids on his face.

He shouldn't have worried. Both men reeked of booze and didn't look as though they were up to making a single discerning observation.

"You seen it?" one of them asked him as he looked into John's eyes. His were watery and vague. He was the taller of the two and reed thin. His face was covered with gray stubble. The other was shorter and younger by a decade, but both were easily drinking away pensions. They were dressed more or less alike in heavy jackets, jeans, boots and cowboy hats.

"Seen what?" John asked. He had the feeling he'd come in late to a show that was already in progress.

"My truck," the tall one said, burying his hands in his pockets.

John stared at the old guy a second, trying to figure out if this was a joke. He finally repeated, "Your truck?"

The old man held out unsteady hands as though to demonstrate how big the truck was. "It's black," he muttered.

"Hell, it's mostly rust," the other guy sniggered.

The old man looked offended for a second, then emitted a loud guffaw. "Someone must of stole it," he said.

"Who would steal that pile of—"

"Well, it's not here, is it?" the thin one barked, kicking at the muddy parking lot and almost falling on his face. John caught his arm and steadied him.

The younger man studied the empty spot and shook his head. "It sure ain't."

John looked around the lot to see if they'd parked it somewhere else and forgotten about it—not that he would tell them. Neither was in any condition to drive. It turned out to be a moot point as there was no rusty black truck in sight.

"Let me ask you a question," John said. "Have either of you seen a large man in a gold car with a young blonde woman? Would have been in the last couple of hours, probably less—"

He shut up as he registered their blank expressions. Identical shakes of their heads followed, and John knew he was wasting time.

"Damn thief," the older guy said. Looking at his friend, he added, "Now how are we going to get home?"

"Come on, George, it'll be A-OK, hunky-dory. What we need is a little drink. Come on."

The two men swung their arms around each other and tottered off.

John's mind raced as he stared at their retreating forms. There was another possibility: What if Korenev had stolen the truck? It would be a perfect cover. Who would suspect a murderer to be driving a wreck like that, and the vehicle itself would be a piece of cake to hot-wire. It wouldn't be fitted with alarms, either....

If that's what had happened, where was the Pollocks' vehicle? It wasn't in the lot, that was for sure.

And where was Paige? Would Anatola Korenev really stick her in an old truck with him?

He yelled across the lot. "Hey, was there a camper or a shell on the back of your truck?"

The older man paused and turned. He appeared to be thinking.

"Hell, no," the younger one said, tugging on the older one's arm. They resumed their unsteady advance on the tavern.

Time was ticking away and John didn't know what to do except keep driving, hoping that Korenev had taken the truck and it had fallen apart close by.

He got back in Paige's car and started circling the tavern to exit. That's when he saw a few broken branches on the trees at the back of the lot. Was that a road beneath them?

No. He accelerated again, but at the last minute, he looked back over his shoulder and slowed the car. The cracks in the branches looked starkly white against the dark wood. New cracks.

He slammed on the brakes and tore open his door. Running into the trees, he followed what appeared to be a trail of mangled undergrowth and rutted wet dirt until he caught a glimpse of gold paint: the tail end of the Pollocks' car.

His heart banged against his ribs as he fought

his way through the brushwood until he could peer inside.

Paige's purse and wallet lay on the floor. Bending and twisting, he retrieved them, stuffed them in his pocket and tried to figure out what it meant.

Had she been forced into an old black truck at knifepoint and driven away? Or had she been murdered, her body tossed aside within these woods?

He shuddered at the daunting scope of searching a whole forest. It was time to call in the cops. What happened to him didn't matter—he'd thought he could handle this alone, but it was obvious now he couldn't. He ran back out of the forest and approached Paige's car. When he paused to open the door, he heard a noise above the sound of his own ragged breathing.

He turned around so quickly he stumbled back against the fender. Holding his breath and straining to hear, he waited—there it was again, a thumping sound. But where was it coming from?

The sound stopped and for a minute or so, he thought he was going crazy, that he was making things up, that maybe bashing his head on the rocks the day before had unhinged him—

No, there it was again, coming from back

near the trees to the left. He began walking that direction, pausing to listen once or twice.

There were two or three older cars back there that looked as though they hadn't moved in a while. As he approached, he noticed pieces of red plastic on the ground beneath a hole where the right taillight had been on an old red sedan. As John watched, something appeared in the opening and then fell, stopping short—

It took him a dumbfounded second to finally realize he was staring at a gold-and-silver pendant hanging from a slender chain. An owl. Paige's owl in all its unsettling glory.

He ran the last few steps and pounded on the trunk. "Paige?" The owl necklace fell to the ground as though dropped in startled clumsiness. "Paige, hold on, I'll get you out of there."

He heard the reassuring sound of a muffled voice.

He moved around to the driver's door but it was locked. Through the window, he could see the passenger door was open a bit, and he hurried around the car. Careful to avoid the broken window glass, he easily found the opener in the cleaned-out glove box and pushed it.

As he lifted the truck lid, his brain registered a slew of details. Paige lay all scrunched up with her back to the rear of the car, a leather strap around her neck. Her hands were taped together, as were her ankles. It appeared she'd managed to wield a tire iron and had used it to bang out the taillight, working with her back to the job. He had no idea how she managed to manipulate the necklace from around her neck let alone dangle it through the opening.

He lifted her out of the trunk. Her eyes were wide, her gaze darting all around as though searching for a sign of Korenev. At first she couldn't stand without John's help. He lifted what he now saw was a man's leather belt from over her head and tossed it back in the trunk, flinching at the angry red burn that encircled her throat. Apologizing ahead of time, he peeled the tape away from her mouth, and she cried out as it lifted from her lips.

He pulled her against him. "Are you all right? Did he hurt you?"

"No. Not really," she mumbled.

"Where is he?"

She looked over his shoulder, then met his gaze. "I don't know. I felt his weight shift as he got out of the car. I kept waiting…waiting for him to come back, you know. There was a sound by the trunk as though he paused, but then voices across the lot and retreating footsteps. Someone must have spooked him. I heard an engine start nearby. That's when I started bashing out the taillight. I didn't know if you would come—"

"Of course I came. I'm sorry it took so long."

She pushed herself away. Her eyes were moist. "I've never been so scared in my life."

He swallowed a boulder as his gaze took in the split skin over her cheekbone and the chalky white of her complexion. She looked away from him—what was she thinking? She'd heard Korenev's accusations. She must be wondering if he was as ruthless as Korenev.

"Could you get this tape off of me?" she asked.

"Of course." He freed her hands and then knelt before her to unwind the silver adhesive from her legs. It seemed to take forever.

"What do we do now?" she asked as she rubbed her hands together as if trying to re-establish circulation. Staring at the ground, she added, "Do you see my necklace? I dropped it."

"It's right here," he said, and gestured at the glittering gold that had fallen through the mushy snow and lay now among a dozen jagged pieces of red plastic.

He bent to pick it up for her and paused.

Although the pendant's topaz eyes were no bigger than decorative pinheads, they still managed to drill right inside his head. For a microsecond, his skin seemed on fire, and then it was over. He wiped a thin layer of perspiration off his forehead. He was crazy. There was no other explanation.

Without saying a word, she picked up the owl and chain, examined it for a second and dropped it into her pocket where it disappeared from sight.

He took a deep breath.

"I had to break it to get it off my neck," she murmured, and once again he looked at the burn on her lovely throat. He'd thought it came from Korenev's bondage methods, but now he saw the abrasion was too narrow for the belt to have caused it. It was yanking on the chain that had burned her skin. *It was the owl...*

"You have a black eye," he said, gently touching her left cheek and willing himself to stop being such an unmitigated sissy.

"We match. We can tell people we've been in a car accident."

He stared into her troubled gray eyes and felt himself drifting toward her. He gave a mental shake of his head and murmured something about getting out of the lot before someone noticed them.

She looked over his shoulder, then back with a startled expression on her face. "You mean someone like that?"

He turned to see what she meant. A police car rolled slowly down the street.

"Hurry," she said as she grabbed his lapels and pulled him toward her. "Kiss me."

He did not need any more invitation than that, and immediately took her up on her suggestion. Her lips were cool and fresh and yet warm, too, and so soft.

It was a brief kiss and he knew its purpose was to dissuade a cop from investigating them closer, but it was also the most wonderful thing that had happened to him in twenty-four hours. It connected him with another person in a way that fused the crevices of his soul, like pouring warm water on a block of ice.

It was over in a few short seconds, and he stared down at her as she checked out the street behind him. Her profile was beautiful, her lashes long and luxuriant.

"They're gone," she said. "We should leave before they come back."

"Or Korenev does," he added. As he led her to her car, he told her about the roadblock. "You leave me here and drive out the main way. You'll run into the police in about ten miles and then you'll be safe."

"What about you?"

He shook his head. The truth: he was loath to see her go. It felt wonderful to have her beside him again, to not be alone. He didn't want to lose her in the worst way possible.

But he couldn't stand the thought she might run into Korenev again because of him.

"John? You can't get out of here on foot. We'll stick together for now, okay?"

"No. Absolutely not."

"I don't want to be by myself," she said, and now for the first time, her voice trembled. "Don't make me drive off alone, please. If you want me to go to the cops, then come with me."

"I can't. I have to find out who and what I am."

"I know you do. So, get in the car. I'll drive to make it all legal, although my wallet is back in the Pollocks' car." She hugged herself as she added, "I really don't want to go back into that forest."

"You don't have to," he said and pulled her things from his pocket. She took them gratefully. Fingering the blue leather wallet with the strangest expression on her face, she looked up at him. "You said that for better or worse, we were in this together. Did you mean it?"

"Absolutely. But—"

"Then let's get out of here."

Chapter Six

Paige clutched the steering wheel with sweaty, shaky hands. Some sort of delayed reaction had begun to erupt inside her. It was all she could do not to turn around and go find the cop whom she'd been so cavalier about only minutes before.

She sneaked a glance at John, who was tinkering with the GPS that came with the car. She'd used it only once and that was to find her way to the mountains a few days earlier. Then she'd been alone and heartbroken but by comparison with how she now felt, her former condition seemed downright lighthearted.

She glanced at John again. "Can you make sense of that thing?" she asked.

"Yeah. Don't ask me how. It looks like there's a subsidiary road a few miles south of here that goes east through the mountains. It's roundabout. In fact, it will make a four- or five-hour trip into one three times as long, but should work."

"Sounds good."

"It's probably unpaved, you know. It could be hard on your car."

"That can't be helped. It's our only alternative."

There she went again. Of course it wasn't *her* only alternative. She could take John up on his offer. She could drive off by herself and find a whole bevy of policemen. She chose to be in this vehicle with John Cinca, sharing this danger, and the reason for that completely baffled her.

Unless— Was this some kind of irrational in-your-face payback to Brian because he'd humiliated her? He'd thought he'd ruined her life. He'd begged her forgiveness even as his gaze kept straying to his ex, Jasmine.

All Paige had wanted was to disappear off the face of the earth. No, that's not true. She'd wanted Brian and Jasmine to disappear, too.

So now she was risking life and limb for another good-looking guy with a hard-luck story. And this one could be a cold-blooded murderer like Anatola Korenev, because it was obvious the two men shared some kind of history.

"You've gotten pretty quiet," John said.

"I was thinking."

"Dare I ask what about?"

"You."

He grunted. "You're wondering why you insisted on sticking with me."

"Sort of," she said. "Nothing that has happened since we met has been rational."

He seemed to study the cuts on the insides of his hands as he thought. "Not on the surface," he finally said, looking up at her. "But that's probably because we don't have the facts."

"If your memory would just come back—"

"Oh, please," he said, holding up a hand and cringing. "Be careful what you wish for. Hearing Anatola Korenev insinuate I'm a murderer worries the hell out of me."

"He was yanking your chain."

"I hope so."

"John? What are you going to do when you get off this mountain?"

"I've been thinking about that. The television people said I was a bodyguard from Lone Tree, right? So my plan is to go there and look myself up. See what I can find. But first I'm going to make sure you arrive home in one piece. I don't know if Korenev can get out of these mountains without being caught, but there's something about the man that screams determination. At least Korenev doesn't know who you are."

"Yes, he does. He looked at my driver's license."

"Great." He shook his head. "Now he has your name and address."

She tried to hide the shiver that pricked her skin. "He doesn't know where I live. He doesn't even know the right town. The address on my driver's license is three years old. I've moved twice since then. I live in Parker now, not Casper."

"That's good news," he said. He paused for a second before adding, "What exactly did Korenev say to you? Did he talk about me?"

"Just in a roundabout way. He alluded to the fact you and he had business to conduct. And then he wanted to know how you and I knew each other. I said we really didn't."

"Good."

"Well, then I got to thinking my chances at surviving might be improved if he thought I was important to you, so I told him we were lovers."

He cast her an incredulous expression. "And he bought that?"

"I think so."

"That I fell down a waterfall and happened to meet my girlfriend in a cabin nearby?"

"I can be a pretty convincing liar," she said. "Anyway, he mentioned he was in a hurry a couple of times, so maybe he decided it didn't really matter."

"Did he say why he was in a hurry?"

"No. On the other hand, he'd just murdered two people and kidnapped another, so it makes sense he'd be antsy. Or how about this: maybe he knew you were up here to meet with someone, and he assumed it was me."

"Up here to meet someone," he repeated. "If that's true, who? No, don't bother to say it. There is no answer." He sighed. "Okay, I officially want my memory back. I'll take whatever I have coming to me, but stumbling around in the dark sucks."

"Don't pay me any attention," Paige said, alarmed with how upset her suggestion had made him. "I'm just talking off the top of my head."

"But there's something to be said for it. For one thing, Anatola Korenev said he walked down the mountain instead of tumbling down the waterfall like I apparently did. We know he didn't have a car waiting at the bottom because he stole the Pollocks'. The news report mentioned two cars in the park where the man was beaten. One was registered to me. One was stolen and abandoned. And yet there had to be three of us up there at the same time. Me, the guy who got beat up and Anatola."

"What are you saying? That you went up there with one of them or the other?"

"Or met them both there. It's obvious the meeting didn't have anything to do with camping." He stared at his hands again and shook his head.

What must it be like not to remember what had gone on inside your own brain just twenty-four hours before? Terrifying, especially when evidence suggested none of it was very nice. "In the end he left me in the trunk," she said, "so I guess he had second thoughts about my story."

"I think it was more than that. The next easiest vehicle in that lot to hot-wire was the old truck with zilch places to hide you all taped up and gagged. How could he explain you if someone stopped him?"

She didn't answer. She couldn't. For a second she was back in that trunk, in the dark and cold. She heard the grinding of an engine that wouldn't start, then the bounce of the tired springs as Korenev got out of the car. And voices. Maybe he'd been ready to kill her before he left and paused because someone noticed him. All she knew was the relief she'd felt as his footsteps retreated.

"You sure you don't want me to drive?" John asked.

She glanced at him and he pointed at the rearview mirror. Three cars trailed behind her.

"It's better if we don't draw attention to ourselves," he added softly.

Paige pulled the car over. It was as though all the bones in her body had dissolved and left her limp and washed out to the point where even pushing down on the accelerator pedal was taxing. They changed places.

"What road are we looking for?" she asked as they passed a cluster of houses.

"Territorial 4001."

"The sign said it's a mile up ahead."

Territorial 4001 started out good but turned bad fast, going from gravel to dirt to deeply rutted within a few miles. Worse, the elevation climbed and the snow on the ground grew more pronounced. They pushed on, though it was impossible not to wonder if it would get too deep before the end.

"Is there anything up ahead?" John asked. "A town or something?"

She scanned the GPS screen. "It looks like there's a place called Soda Valley about ten miles from here."

"Hopefully it's big enough to warrant plowing the road if it gets too snowy," he said as the car seemed to sink to its bumper in a pothole. "Sorry."

Paige tried to wedge herself into the seat to avoid the bouncing and jarring, but just as the adrenaline had left her body, the aches and pains caused by all the throwing, shoving and thumps she'd endured had arrived with a vengeance.

Her kingdom for an aspirin.

Even if she had one, there was no water with which to take it or with which to wash off some of the blood and grime. And suddenly she was hungry. It had been a long time since breakfast. A year, maybe. Perhaps two....

"I want to stop in Soda Valley," she said. "I'm starving, aren't you?"

"Now that you mention it," he said.

SODA VALLEY TURNED OUT to be nestled in a small basin. The snow was deeper here but the roads had been plowed and sanded. John kept his concerns to himself, but he did comfort himself that Paige's car had both all-wheel drive and chains in the trunk. He had a feeling they would need both before they cleared the mountains.

The town itself was larger than he'd expected but was still a one-street town about six blocks long. He kept his eyes peeled for an old black truck as he pulled into a gas station. Paige used her credit card, and once the tank was full they continued into the heart of the "city," where John parked against the curb.

Turning to Paige, he asked if she could loan him some money.

"How much?"

"Ten or twenty bucks? I assume I can repay you eventually."

She opened her wallet. "All I have is two fifties. You take one, I'll take the other. I'm going to go find food and water and aspirin. What are you going to do?"

"I'm going to find something warmer and less conspicuous to wear."

"Okay. Meet me back here in twenty minutes?"

"Deal. But Paige," he added, catching her arm. "Keep your eyes open for you know who."

She went off one direction and he took the other, doing his best to blend in, but the curious glances thrown his way suggested it was a lost cause. He felt as if he was wearing a sign that announced he was a wanted man.

At the end of the third block he found a thrift shop. There wasn't a lot to choose from, but he quickly settled on cowboy boots that were just a little tight but still had most of their soles, a pair of faded, worn denim jeans, a blue flannel shirt and a vest to cover the gun and holster. The only coat he could find was heavy and woolly, but that was fine. It promised warmth and anonymity, and that's what he was after. The real bargain came at the cash register, where he spied a battered knockoff Stetson. The minute he settled it on his head, he felt invisible.

The suit and ruined shoes got rolled into a ball. Detouring off the main street, he found a Dumpster and deposited his old clothes, stuffed inside the thrift-store bag, in among the rest of the refuse.

Paige was already back in the car when he got there, fiddling with her necklace. She'd managed to find somewhere to clean up and had apparently dug through her luggage for a high-collared sweater that covered her neck.

Even after the morning she'd endured, even though her cut cheek was edging toward a black eye, she looked so pretty he had to smile at her. His smile seemed to catch her off guard, and then she looked closer and he realized she hadn't recognized him at first.

"Do I fit in better?" he asked.

"Definitely," she said as she fastened the mended clasp around her neck and tucked the owl beneath her sweater.

They got back into the shelter of the car, and she extracted the biggest sandwich he'd ever seen from a white deli bag. At least he thought it was the biggest he'd seen. How did he know?

She cut the sandwich in half with a little plastic knife, and they sat in the car sharing it. By silent agreement they seemed to have split the chore of looking out for trouble, with Paige staring at the pedestrians on the sidewalk and John keeping an eye on the street.

At the top of the hour, Paige switched on the radio, and with the local news report all semblance of peace flew out the window.

"A retired couple was found murdered in their home late this morning," a woman's voice reported. "Authorities revealed an employee of Haskins Satellite came across the bodies of a man and woman at their Woodside Street home when he kept a prearranged appointment to install equipment. Police have not yet released the identity of the couple or the exact circumstances of the killings except to say robbery may have been the motive.

"There is speculation that the murders may be linked to yesterday's ruthless attack of an unidentified man who is still in a coma. Wanted for questioning in that situation is Lone Tree bodyguard John Cinca, who remains at large. The public is encouraged to contact authorities if they have any information and to consider Cinca armed and dangerous."

They had both stopped eating as they listened and now looked at each other. John tried to read Paige's expression but he couldn't. Once again, he was amazed she'd stuck with him this long. Why had she? What could be her motive?

Was it possible she was part of this? Was it possible he'd come to these mountains to meet her, that she was in cahoots with Anatola Korenev and that she was playing him?

He stared at the high collar of her sweater....

"John?"

Startled by her voice, he jerked, met her gaze and looked away.

"Please don't worry about that report," she said. "I know for sure you didn't kill Jack and Carolyn, and I know for sure Anatola Korenev did. This will all work out, trust me."

Trust her. That's what it was all about, and if anyone in that car was walking the line of sanity when it came to extending trust, it wasn't him—it was her.

He began stuffing leftovers into the bag. The small town of Soda Valley suddenly seemed full of prying eyes, the interior of the car far too intimate. Paige shook an aspirin into her hand and took a drink from a water bottle.

"I could use a couple of those, too," he said and held out his hand.

THEY SOON CLIMBED OUT of the meadow and wound around a tall hill, the snow on each side of the plowed road growing so deep in places it felt as though they were driving through a tunnel of ice.

"Tell me about Brian," John said after a half hour of silence. It had just begun to snow again and there was no other traffic on the road. Paige, sitting in the passenger seat, had settled into a kind of numb trance, staying awake just because the images when she closed her eyes were so jarring.

Not that hearing Brian's name wasn't unsettling in its own way. "What about him?"

"What does he do? What does he look like? How did you meet?"

As she spoke, she stared at the windshield wipers knocking off the snow.

"He's blond with blue eyes," she began. "Tall, athletic, handsome. He's in advertising. We met when I was asked to design a cover for a pamphlet his company was promoting."

"Love at first sight?"

"Attraction, but not love. He was still married. I didn't agree to date him until the final decree came through."

"Did he want the divorce?"

"He was actually really broken up about it."

"Why?"

Paige shrugged. "She'd cheated on him with a good friend and he felt totally abandoned by everyone. He would have stayed with her if she'd let him despite her infidelity. She called all the shots."

John cast her a wry smile. "Sound familiar?"

She stared at his profile. He wasn't as classically good-looking as Brian, nor as smooth, and she liked that. He appeared to be genuine in a way that defied the fact he wasn't sure who or what he was. And the few seconds where their lips had touched had produced an alluring sizzle she was curious to investigate.

"No," she said. "You are not like Brian. He was looking for someone to fill a sudden void—"

John cleared his throat. "Please, forget I asked, okay?"

"He made the first move," she continued. "He pursued me right up until the moment when his ex-wife crooked her finger and invited him back. That is not you. You are not interested in me that way. In fact, you are constantly trying to get rid of me."

He cast her a swift look and a crooked smile. "That's not entirely true."

Radio reception had disappeared the minute they left the valley, so they couldn't keep abreast of the manhunt that was apparently afoot for John. They fell into silence again until the snow got so thick the wipers had a hard time keeping up with it.

"It's going to be dark soon," John said, slow-ing the car and pulling as far to the side of the road as he dared. "I think we should get the chains on before it's too late."

"I don't know how to put the chains on," Paige said. "I was counting on a brand-spanking-new husband to do it for me when and if we needed them."

"I'll play husband and put them on. You stay in here. Won't take me long."

But she got out of the car with him, partly because he might need help, partly because it was her car and she felt responsible for it, and partly because she was afraid she'd fall asleep if she didn't. As he struggled with the chains, she stood by, snuggled deep in her coat and cold despite it. *John must be miserable down on the ground like that.*

Invariably, her thoughts turned to the Pollocks. Somehow she felt better knowing their bodies had been found and any relatives notified of their terrible fates. It had felt categorically wrong to leave them like that.

How many laws had she broken today? Aiding a suspected criminal? Not reporting violent deaths? Probably something to do with knocking out the taillight in that old wreck…

How many crimes had she committed up to this point in her life? She'd walked on the grass a few times when signs warned her not to, and let's face it, sometimes she drove too fast and was late getting a library book back on time. But that was the extent of her criminal activity.

Until now.

Eventually, John got the chains on and they scooted back into the relative warmth of the car. As John started the engine, Paige turned the heater on full blast. He checked the GPS. "You should be home by early morning," he said as he pulled back onto the road. The world outside the car was white and gray and nothing else.

"Home," she said softly.

"Don't you want to go home?"

"It'll be the first time I've seen everyone since I had to tell them there wasn't going to be a wedding," she said. "So, no, I'm not really looking forward to it."

"Your friends and family will shower you with concern," he said in an obvious attempt at comforting her.

"I know. They'll smother me with kindness. *Kindness.* Who am I trying to kid. It's pity they'll shower me with, and who could blame them? But honestly, who wants to be pitied?"

"Not you," he said.

"No, not me. I share an apartment with my younger sister, Katy. She may have already rented out my room. I packed all my stuff in preparation for moving in with Brian. Most of it's at his place, or at least it was. I wonder what he did with it. I may be going home to nothing."

"But your sister was at your wedding, right? She knows what happened."

"For all I know, she may have rented my room out before the wedding," Paige said. "Katy is pretty adept at looking out for Katy. No way can she afford the rent all by herself."

"Wouldn't she tell you if she'd done that?"

"I was so busy with wedding details that I barely saw her for weeks before the wedding. And I might as well be honest. We don't always get on so great. She's a tad on the head-strong side."

"Must run in your family," he said, grinning.

"Ha-ha."

"How about your parents?"

"Mother lives locally, Father is a retired fire-man who currently resides in Alaska."

"You could move back with your mother—"

"Oh, no, please, you don't know what you're saying. Mom is in the process of wooing hus-band candidate number four. I do not want to get anywhere near that train wreck."

"How about your father? If you're a graphic artist, you can work almost anywhere at least for a while, can't you?"

"Technically, but I have a lot of local clients." She sighed. "I've always been closer to my father than my mother. I guess I could fly up to Alaska and stay with him for a couple of weeks, but what does that get me? Sooner or later, I have to reclaim my disaster of a life. Might as well get it over with."

She flashed John a smile she didn't feel. The truth she would never admit out loud was she would rather stay with him. She didn't know why, but his journey seemed a lot more important than anything she had planned for the next few days, weeks, months....

And she wanted to make sure Anatola Korenev paid for what he'd done to the Pollocks. He could not be allowed to wreck more lives.

Paige Graham, seeker of justice for the dead.

Cripes, she thought. *I am totally delusional.*

She must have said it aloud, because John laughed.

Chapter Seven

A glance at the dashboard clock revealed the reason John kept finding his eyes drifting shut. It was three in the morning, and he was so tired he was a hazard on the road. Two or three times he startled awake after a few seconds of nodding off to find the car had wandered into the wrong lane. Good thing there was no one else out tonight.

The plowed roads had stopped at a small town they drove through an hour before, and now his were the only tracks on the newly fallen snow. Thankfully it wasn't deep as they had steadily been losing elevation, but it was tricky driving and dangerous in his condition as the road wove its way through the trees.

He finally found what appeared to be a grove of some kind of fir trees where the snow wasn't too deep and he pulled in, telling himself even an hour of sleep would recharge his battery.

Paige had been out for the count since midnight, and he hoped the stop wouldn't wake her.

They were both bundled up, but he knew the car would get cold and figured that cold would act as an alarm clock. Not that he really cared. He had to sleep.

The dream started pleasantly enough. He strolled by a stream in the sunlight. Someone was with him but he wasn't sure who it was. And then black shadows stole across the sky, turning day into night. He was sitting in a dark room next. All around him he could hear the rustle of wings. Birds. Dozens of them, just vague shadows and deep noises—owls! The bird sounds were suddenly joined by screams and not just any screams, children's screams of terror. They were terrified of the owls, too. He tried to sink into the earth to get away from the wings and the cries. His hands were covered with blood and his body was on fire....

"John!"

He opened his eyes. Paige leaned over him, eyes wide with alarm.

He swallowed heavily and tried to sit up but he'd slipped down in the seat in his twilight attempt to escape the owls, pinning his hip under the steering wheel. He maneuvered himself upright and took another gulp of cold air.

"Are you all right?" she asked, her hand landing on his arm.

"Yeah," he said. The truth was more complicated as the dream continued to unwind in the back of his head.

"You were screaming," she said. He suddenly realized it was daylight. Condensation on the inside of the windows made the outside world a blur.

"I was? Sorry."

"Were you having a nightmare?"

"Yes," he said, and rubbed his eyes. The beating of wings grated against every nerve ending. He met her gaze and looked away. If it was possible to feel like a raw sore, he did.

"You look funny, John. Do you want to talk about it?"

"No," he said. He didn't know what to make of the crying children.

He opened the driver's door and stumbled from the seat into a foot of snow. Judging from the light filtering through the treetops, it was early morning.

Paige came up behind him and circled him with her arms. At first, the gesture made him uneasy. Why was she hugging him? Why was she with him? He turned around to face her.

"You look so lost," she said.

"And you're a sucker for wounded guys,

right?" The owl pendant was beneath her sweater. He couldn't see it, but he could sense it there. The metal wings beating against her skin, the yellow eyes burning through the wool.

"Maybe," she said. "Is that so wrong?"

"It can be," he said, raising his gaze to her eyes.

"Why?"

"If it impairs your judgment," he said. "If it puts you in danger."

"Not this again," she said, her voice frustrated. "I know what I'm doing."

"Do you, Paige?"

"You're not dangerous," she said.

"I'm not? Are you sure?" He grabbed her shoulders and pulled her close to him. Staring into her eyes, fueled by the residue of the nightmare amped up by unbearable uncertainty, he touched her lips with his, then drew back, startled by the almost audible clap of thunder that resonated in his head.

Thunder that drove away the beating wings and the cries...

He claimed her lips again. As chaste as the kiss in the tavern parking lot had been, this one was wanton, bordering on licentious. His hands slid up her neck, his fingers splayed through her hair as he pried her lips open with the tip of his tongue. His mind was blessedly free of sounds other than the rushing of his own blood, the pumping of his own heart.

It was Paige. She was the reason he was free…. And as inappropriate and impossible the situation, all he wanted was to pull her to the snowy ground and lose himself in her.

His hand slid down her back, cupped her butt, tucked her tight against his groin—

For a second, his head cleared and he stood back from himself. Then he pushed her away, appalled by his behavior. Her swollen lips and dazed eyes bore testimony to the way he'd transferred his angst to her. That was the last thing in the world he wanted to do.

"Paige, I—"

"Don't say anything," she pleaded, pressing her fingertips against her mouth. "Please, not a word."

"But—"

"We should go. I'll drive."

She practically darted back to the car and slid in behind the wheel without looking at him again.

He didn't want to get in her car. He didn't want to be anywhere near her. His head was pounding now as the children's screams took on substance—

He was the fiend in his nightmare. He was

the reason they cried…. He walked around and opened the passenger door.

He must not hurt Paige.

PAIGE PLANTED BOTH HANDS on the wheel and kept her focus straight ahead. The road soon descended with a series of twists and turns to where they finally cleared the trees. A couple of hours later, she drove into a small town and stopped at a gas station. She was less than a hundred miles from home now. The thought of reentering her own life suddenly appealed to her in a way it hadn't before.

The truth of that kiss was that it was her fault. She'd known from the moment John woke up that something about him was different, as if he'd gone to sleep one man and woken up another. Still, she'd pushed herself on him, anxious to help.

When this whole thing was over, she needed to find herself a good head doctor and figure out who she was, because the Paige Graham currently running amok bore little resemblance to the Paige Graham who had been on the verge of marrying Brian Witherspoon. It was time to back off.

But, wow, that must have been some nightmare.

John disappeared inside the station while she

bought gas. Maybe he was planning to go his own way, hitch a ride or walk. That would be for the best. Things were out of control.

The attendant gave her a key and she used the restroom to clean herself up. Still, her sister, Katy, was going to be more than a little surprised when Paige showed up all bruised and cut and in clear need of a shower. Hopefully she wouldn't call their mother and start some kind of drama. No more drama, please. The debacle of the wedding and the past twenty-four hours were quite enough for one decade.

John was sitting in the passenger seat when she returned to the car. He had a bag full of bagels, he muttered, and two cups of coffee. *Bon appétit*.

But she was hungry and she accepted what he offered and ate as she drove on the lovely clear highway with lots of other people around. The horror of the day before receded a little.

He waited until after they'd eaten to tune in the radio. As it was, it took a few minutes for the news to come on and when it did, it was full of a rehash of yesterday's grisly find. The Pollocks were referred to by name this time, and Paige felt the last tendrils of guilt unwrap themselves from around her heart. It was all out in the open now.

Except, they were still looking for John. That

didn't mean they weren't looking for Korenev, as well—the police didn't always release every detail they knew. The news did mention finding the Pollocks' car near Gil's Tavern. That meant they would also find Anatola Korenev's blood smeared all over the place.

The last unsettling comment came at the end of the report when it was mentioned that a honeymooning couple by the name of Brian and Paige Witherspoon, who had been renting a cabin in the mountains in the same general area as the Pollocks, could not be located and that there were signs of a struggle and a macabre find in the freezer.

"They don't know I was up there alone," she said. "And now they think Brian and I are both missing. I should have thought of that."

"I didn't think of it either," John said as she switched off the radio. He groaned as he added, "My prints must be on file somewhere and they have to be all over your cabin."

"But Anatola Korenev's might be there, too, and his will be in the Pollocks' car, as well. Yours won't. Will they? Did you touch it when you got my stuff?"

"I must have touched the handle. Damn."

"I should notify my family I'm okay."

"And Brian, too."

"Brian can tell the police whatever he wants.

I am not getting involved with him again. Period. By the way, what do you think they meant when they said there was a macabre find in the freezer? I might have left some ice cream behind...."

"It wasn't you," John said, casting her a quick glance. "I actually stuck Korenev's finger up there."

"You what?"

"His severed finger. It'll have a print that might match some in the car, right?"

She stared at him for a second, then put her attention back on the road, but a second later, she started laughing and couldn't seem to quit.

She pulled over as soon as she could and called her mother, who wasn't home. No doubt she was at the gym where she taught yoga classes. Paige didn't want to call the gym. She left a message assuring her mother she was fine and would talk to her soon.

"If the police think you're missing, they may be waiting at your apartment," John said as they drove into Parker. He darted glances out the windows, probably looking for the cops.

"I guess. I don't know how that works, although from what I've read in the newspaper, I don't think the police department can afford stakeouts. For all they know, Brian and I drove off to California or for that matter, if they've found out that we didn't get married, they'll probably assume I drove off to pout."

"Yeah," he said. "Maybe."

The drive ended at Paige's apartment building, or what she hoped would still be her apartment building. John caught her wrist as she turned off the ignition, releasing it immediately.

"I want to apologize," he said.

"Don't worry about it."

"No, Paige, don't brush me off, please."

She stared at him for a few seconds. His bruises had gone from black-and-blue to a shade of green she knew her own would soon achieve. The cuts were mending. The bandage on his chin had fallen off. Dressed in the cowboy duds, he looked like a bank robber who had ridden all night to escape a lynching posse, which, come to think of it, pretty much described the situation. The frightening look of before was gone. His eyes were calm now, his features less sharp.

Despite everything, her heart went out to him.

Man, she was a sucker.

She ran her hands over her eyes. They burned with fatigue. "Okay."

"I think I had a kind of hangover from the nightmare."

"Explain."

He swallowed and rubbed the back of his

neck. "I dreamed about owls. And screaming children."

"What do you mean screaming children?"

"I couldn't see them. There were just these voices and terrible cries.... After I...after I kissed you I realized the screams were accusations directed at me. I was on fire, like I was in hell. That's what it felt like: hell. The only escape seemed to be you."

He stopped talking abruptly and took a deep breath. Paige flashed on the old burn scars on his back and legs.

"I awoke feeling like I'd had the dream before, maybe many times," he added. "I'm a killer, Paige. I'm sure of it."

He swallowed again and Paige winced at the pain on his face. "Maybe it means you were a soldier in a war," she said. "Or that you were a firefighter and couldn't save a child."

"Or maybe I'm just plain out nuts. If the police arrest me now, I'll end up in some kind of mental institution."

They could get adjoining rooms...

"So go home, John, before the police or Anatola Korenev find you. Go home and see if walking in your own space jars you back to yourself. Find out about your past—it will explain all this."

"I hope you're right."

She stared at him a second, then shook her head and stared down at her hands. "You weren't the only one to blame," she said softly. "About the kiss, I mean. I knew you were acting all spacey. And it's not like it wasn't a hell of a kiss."

He smiled. "I think you're accepting responsibility you don't deserve," he said, "but thanks for the gesture. And I promise you, nothing like that will ever happen again."

"We've had a strange relationship right from the start," she said slowly. Staring at him, a thought occurred that hadn't before. "Lone Tree is only about fifty miles from here, right?" she added.

"I think so."

"I'm driving you," she said firmly, and held up a hand to still his protest. "Don't argue. You can't get on a bus or hitchhike or take a train—someone will recognize you. It's only an hour drive for me. But first I have to go upstairs and at least leave a note for Katy so she doesn't freak out when she hears the radio."

"What about the police?"

"I think I should get you back to Lone Tree before I call them. Might save on answering some really hard questions. I'll be back in a minute. Katy is usually home at this time of the day, but you never know."

"I'm coming with you," he said.

"Do you think that's a good idea? Wouldn't it be better to stay out of sight?"

"You've forgotten about Anatola Korenev," he said softly.

"But he doesn't know where I live," she said.

"If he listens to the radio, he can figure it out after that last report."

"But how could he get off the mountain before us?"

"I don't know. Maybe he didn't. Do you want to bet your life on it?"

"No."

He flipped open his vest and pulled the gun from its holster. "The media says I'm a bodyguard. Time I earned my keep." He pulled the cowboy hat down low on his forehead and opened his door. "Stay behind me."

THE APARTMENT BUILDING WAS relatively new but it had zero security at the front door that opened directly into a hallway. Paige lived on the ground floor at the end of the left passage. At the sight of her front door standing wide open, Paige broke into a run and avoided John's grab for her arm as she ran past him.

"Katy?" she screamed.

John arrived a microsecond after her, swearing internally. It seemed Paige was determined to face every horrific sight before he could possibly shield her. But this time, although chaos abounded, there didn't seem to be a dead, mutilated body anywhere.

"Let me check the bedrooms," he said, and she backed up against the wall and stood there, eyes wide with fear at what he might discover.

John stepped over half-empty boxes and stacks of clothes, dishes, books and everything in between. Had Korenev been here, searching for something to help him find Paige or John?

The first bedroom held nothing but two boxes stacked in the corner and taped shut. The adjoining bathroom was equally clean. The next bedroom was even more frenzied than the living area; ditto for the bathroom.

He put his gun away and walked into the living area, where he hastily assured Paige her sister wasn't dead or injured somewhere else in the apartment. She sagged at the knees with relief and stepped over things to meet him in the middle of the mess.

"What if Korenev came in here and took her?" she said.

John put his arms around her, and she buried her head against his chest for a second. "I have to call the police," she mumbled into his jacket. "I'll have to tell them everything I know. I have to get Katy back. I'm sorry."

He tilted her chin up and gazed into her moist eyes, drawing his fingers across her cheeks to wipe away the tears. "Of course you do. Don't worry—"

"What the hell is going on?" a female voice interrupted from the hallway. John looked over Paige's head. In one glance he took in a slightly taller, slightly younger version of Paige dressed in tight jeans and a yellow halter top, holding a large roll of plastic tape.

Paige turned at the sound of the voice. "Katy!" she screamed, and ran toward her sister, jumping over the worst of the mess. "I was so afraid. Thank heavens you're okay."

The two women hugged, then Katy stepped away, tape still clutched in her hand. "What are you doing here? And who is the cowboy?"

"He's just a friend," Paige said with a sideways glance at John before turning her attention back to her sister. "Where were you? Why did you leave the front door wide open?"

"I was upstairs borrowing tape from Matt. Oh my gosh, Paige. Where did you disappear to?"

"Then you heard the news on the radio...."

"What news? I didn't hear anything. I've been buried in here for days. I mean where did you go after the wedding?"

Paige shook her head. "What wedding? Never

mind. Haven't the police contacted you about my whereabouts or maybe Brian's?"

"No. I've been packing. The landline is disconnected and the battery is dead on my cell… Wait! Are you and Brian back together?"

"No. Why are you packing all your stuff?"

Katy rolled her eyes. She might physically resemble Paige but it appeared the likeness ended there. As she spoke, Katy tapped her foot and drummed her fingers against her thigh, as though unable to stay still. Her face was expressive, just like Paige's, but the expressions themselves weren't as beguiling. At least not to him.

"I figured I needed a smaller place," Katy said, "so I rented a studio in that old building downtown. The Palms or something." She plopped next to a box full of books and taped it shut. "I told you this before your wedding. I have to be out of here in two days. And that reminds me. You need to take the rest of your stuff. I guess you'll have to move in with Mom unless you've had a better offer…." Her voice trailed off as she stared at John.

"Katy? Just focus for a second," Paige said. "There was a terrible mess up in the mountains."

Katy looked up from piling blankets in a new box. "What mountains?"

"I went to a cabin in the mountains. You

know, I told you that's where Brian and I were going to honeymoon."

"You went to the cabin all by yourself! Oh, Paige, that's just funny, it really is. Who but you would go off on a honeymoon without a husband?"

"Okay, funny, ha-ha, but there was a killer up there, and I gather the police are concerned I may be a victim, as well."

"So it's going to be all over the news that you went on your honeymoon alone? Man, you're going to be a joke on one of those late-night shows. Does Mom know about this?"

Paige's sigh was audible from six feet away. "No, Mom doesn't know. I left her a message, though. Listen, I'll talk to the cops. You need to leave this apartment right now and not come back until the murderer—"

"Are you crazy?" Katy interrupted with a sweeping gesture of her arm. "I can't leave in the middle of all of this. I have to be out of here tomorrow or I lose my deposit, and I can't afford that. No way."

"This is important."

"You always think your stuff is important," Katy said. "Well, my stuff is important, too. I'll lock the door. Who's going to come looking for you anyway? Besides Brian's uncle, and I told him you were gone and weren't coming back. I knew you didn't want to be involved with any of Brian's lame family and—"

"Wait," Paige said, holding out her hands. "Brian doesn't have an uncle."

"Sure he does. Thick accent? Black beard? Gargantuan eyebrows? Ring any bells? Anyway, me and Matt and Willie G. from across the hall were moving furniture when this dude shows up. He said he'd arrived too late for the wedding and wanted to know when you'd be home. It was like his only chance to meet you or something. I told him you weren't coming back here, I was moving and I didn't know what your plans were. I even let him look around in your room so he could see that I was serious. I didn't really like him. Oh, and I told him his nephew is a jerk-face."

"Was this man's right hand bandaged?" Paige interrupted.

"Yeah. How did you know that?"

"That wasn't Brian's uncle," John said. "When was he here?"

"A couple of hours ago."

"This is the man I've been warning you about," Paige said.

"He's killed at least two people we know of," John added. "He's responsible for the abrasions and cuts on your sister's face and neck."

Katy looked Paige over. "Oh, I didn't notice. You are a mess, aren't you?"

"So, now you'll leave, right?" Paige insisted. "The manager will understand—"

"Mr. Poplin? Are you serious? The only thing he understands is he has a new tenant who wants to move in bright and early tomorrow morning. I still have the whole kitchen to pack and all of this."

"Your life is more important," John said.

Katy propped her hands on her hips and looked from one of them to the other. "You guys are too much, you know that? Are you on drugs or something? Listen, the guy came and he went, big deal. I'll call Matt down to help me and get a couple of guys from work to come over here and stand guard while I finish this up. If the fake uncle shows up again, I'll get Willie G. over here and he'll bore the guy to death. Okay?"

"You don't understand," Paige said with a gentleness that surprised John. How could she be so patient with this woman?

"I understand you think it's important, I really do," Katy said. "I understand this guy is a brute. Got it. But I am finishing this job and getting out of here. I'll leave tonight, I promise, and I won't stay alone. I'm going to go get Matt. Stay here. I'll be right back."

As Katy darted out of the apartment and disappeared down the hall toward the elevators, John took Paige's hands. "You tried."

"I told you she was headstrong."

"You weren't kidding."

"I can't leave her."

"But you can't make her go, either, and now that Korenev has actually seen you don't live here, she's probably safe. Who is this Matt guy?"

"An on-and-off boyfriend of Katy's. He lifts weights and spends every free moment at the gym."

"Do you want to stay with her? I'm fine going on alone."

"There are so many reasons I don't want to stay here I couldn't even begin to list them," Paige said. "She won't listen to me no matter what I say or where I am when I say it."

"Do you want me to get the boxes in the empty room? I assume they're yours."

"That would be great. They're just personal papers. We can stick them in the trunk. For some reason I didn't want to leave them at Brian's place. Now I'm glad I didn't."

John fetched the two boxes. As he reentered the living area, Katy came through the front door with a tall, young guy sporting what appeared to be a salon tan. Muscles bulged in his arms, and his thighs strained against the denim of his jeans. He looked strong enough to bend iron bars with his bare hands.

He produced a shy smile when he saw Paige. "Hey, sorry about the wedding and everything."

Paige nodded. "Thanks, Matt."

"He wasn't good enough for you anyway," Matt said.

She laughed.

"You should have dated me."

"Back off, Romeo. It looks like Paige found herself a cowboy," Katy said with another look at John. "There's a cold beer in the fridge, just like I promised. Bring one for me, too."

"I'm in training. I told you I can't drink beer. You got any of that bottled water with electrolytes and minerals?"

"Maybe. I'll take the beer."

Matt stopped in front of John and extended a hand. John juggled the boxes and returned the gesture, glad the guy didn't feel the need to prove anything by crushing any bones.

"Katy says I'm supposed to keep the hairy guy from coming back in here, right?"

"That's the idea."

Matt's muscles rippled as he pressed his hands together. "Let him try."

"Don't underestimate him," John said. He

lowered his voice and added, "If you can talk Katy into leaving, do it, okay?"

"Sure. Later."

Paige gave Katy a goodbye hug. "You need to call the cops and report a man calling himself Anatola Korenev was at your apartment. They need to know. Please be careful. Lock the door."

"Yeah, yeah."

"And you're going to call some guys from work?"

"Yeah. I'll use Matt's cell. You be careful," Katy added, but she said it with a wink and John got the impression Katy was a lot more concerned about Paige being with him than she was the threat of Anatola Korenev. But for the life of him, he could not see how they could prepare her any more than they had already.

He deposited the boxes in Paige's trunk as she got behind the wheel, steeling himself for the next stage of the journey and what they might find out about him.

"She's not usually quite that oblivious to everything," Paige said as he sat in the passenger seat.

"She's got nerves of steel," he agreed. "Not many women her age would stick around after finding out she'd entertained a killer a few hours before."

"She's a lot like my mother. She can get a... little self-involved."

Like the way she hadn't even noticed how injured Paige was until John pointed it out to her? He kept his mouth shut.

"Anyway," she continued as she pulled away from the curb. "I guess Korenev heard that radio report and figured out where I lived. Sounds like he put on a disguise."

"What's to stop him from also connecting you to Brian Witherspoon? The report said you were married to him. I think you'd better call Brian and make sure he's okay."

She pulled the car over to the side of the road and took her cell phone from her pocket. Then she stared at it. "I know how his brain works," she said at last. "He'll think I'm trying to find out if he's still with Jasmine."

"Really?"

"Super ego when it comes to me."

"Do you want me to make the call?"

"He'll still know it's from my phone."

"Maybe you could leave a message."

"He showers with his cell phone," she said. "He'll answer."

"Let me call. I'll tell him something that lets you off the hook, don't worry."

She punched in a number then handed John the phone. "You're on."

He listened for a minute, then clicked it off.

"Hey," Paige protested. "You said you'd leave a message. Now he'll see I called."

"I couldn't think of anything."

"Drat!"

"You're still hung up on this joker, aren't you?"

"No!"

"Yes, you are. Man, I read you all wrong. Never mind. You said he always answers his phone, but this time he didn't. Maybe he's asleep or something, but you can't forget what Anatola Korenev did to the Pollocks and to you. Drive faster."

She picked up her speed and within ten minutes, they were pulling into a complex of new-looking condos. She parked in front of one that sported a blue convertible in the driveway. At least there were no police cars hanging around. John took a deeper breath. Maybe he'd panicked over nothing.

"You can stay here if you want," he told Paige. "I'll knock on his door, pretend to be an aluminum-siding salesman and just make sure he's in one piece."

"I'm acting like a giant chicken. Let's just get this over with." And with that she opened her door and marched up the path to the front door.

He had to admire her pluck.

HOW MANY HUNDREDS OF TIMES had Paige knocked on Brian's front door? But this was the first time she'd done it while trying not to throw up.

He didn't answer.

And finally, it sunk into her brain that his car was in the driveway and maybe John was right and Brian was in trouble.

"I'm breaking down the door," John said after several tense seconds of waiting.

"Don't," she said, fishing her car keys out of her pocket. She turned to find he once again held the revolver. "I still have his key," she explained.

She used it on the door and opened it slowly, half afraid she would find Brian and his ex in the middle of an orgy on the living-room rug and half afraid she'd find—

"Oh, no," she cried and raced into the apartment, only vaguely aware that John followed close behind.

Brian was on the floor, hands bound behind his back, mouth taped closed, wearing nothing but pajama bottoms. His face bore the same cuts and bruises all of Anatola Korenev's victims eventually sported, and there was a gash across his chest caked with dried blood.

At the sound of their approach, his eyes crept open, his eyelashes fluttered as though he'd been unconscious. His expression went from bewildered to afraid to relieved as he appeared to recognize Paige's face.

She knelt on the floor and took familiar gray duct tape off his mouth while John, setting the handgun on the rug, unwound it from his wrists.

"Paige," Brian mumbled as soon as he could and with his newly freed hands, grabbed her around the waist. He buried his head against her breasts. "Oh my God, Paige. I am so relieved to see you." He pulled her head down and kissed her. "Darling, you will not believe what happened."

A tidal wave of giddiness washed through Paige as the word *darling* echoed through her body. He kissed her again and held her tight. He was hers, she was his, nothing else mattered. She pushed him gently away to search his face, looking for confirmation of this miracle.

She found a black-and-blue knot on his forehead.

"Jasmine," he said, suddenly twisting to look up the stairs. He struggled to get to his feet, and John and Paige each took an arm to help.

"Where is she?" Paige asked. The tidal wave receded as quickly as it had arrived. Too many strong emotions coming too close together left her weak at the knees.

"Upstairs. Oh my God, I sent him up there."

"Sent who?" John asked as though he couldn't guess.

"That man—"

"I'll go check on her," John said, snatching up his gun. He was halfway up the stairs before Brian could protest.

Paige touched Brian's cheek. "Tell me what happened."

His forehead scrunched up as he concentrated. "I heard a noise. Like breaking glass. I came down here to see what was going on. A huge man with a giant beard and thick brows had shattered a glass panel in the French doors and let himself in. He had a knife. He demanded to know where my wife was. He told me she had a new lover, that she was cheating on me. I said, 'No, she doesn't, she's upstairs.'

"That's all I got out. He punched me unconscious. When I came to, he was standing there with my gun. He must have taken it out of the drawer, you know, where I always keep it. He mumbled something about that being the wrong wife, he wanted the one named Paige. I told him where you lived. I just wanted him out of here. I thought I could call you and warn you—I was desperate to check on Jasmine. But he came at me and I fell trying to get away. Must have hit my head on the coffee table, because the next thing I knew you were here and I was gagged."

"Call an ambulance," John shouted from the head of the stairs. "She's alive."

"I've got to go to her," Brian said.

"Go on, I'll make the call," Paige said. As he climbed the stairs, she dialed 911 on his phone and gave them his address.

For a second she just stood there staring at the empty stairs, dreading what she would find when she joined the men. And then it dawned on her that she and John needed to get out of here right away before emergency crews and police showed up. Katy and Brian would both tell about Anatola Korenev, and Brian would mention John—there was no way in the world she could ask him not to.

Things were about to get a heck of a lot more complicated. And if John stood a chance of defending himself properly, he needed facts about his own involvement or complicity.

She called John's name from the foot of the stairs. He responded immediately, leaning over the railing to look down at her.

"Can Brian take care of Jasmine alone until the ambulance gets here?"

"Yes. Korenev beat her up some but he didn't go after her with the knife. Why?"

"I think we should leave."

He glanced over his shoulder at the bedroom, then passed a hand over his eyes that said as eloquently as words how disturbed he was that so many lives had been impacted by whatever situation he was in the middle of. "Are you sure?" he said. "It's beginning to feel like running away."

"I'm positive. There isn't much time. Hurry up."

He joined her downstairs. They left the front door open to facilitate the ambulance crew, then with Paige behind the wheel, exited the pricey housing area by a back road. They both turned in their seats as the sound of an ambulance siren coming from the opposite direction accompanied their departure.

Not long after that, they hit the interstate. Next stop: Lone Tree.

Chapter Eight

"What did Anatola Korenev do to Jasmine?" Paige asked.

John hadn't taken his eyes off the road since they took off. He wasn't sure what he feared most—the police or running into Korenev.

At the sound of Paige's voice he glanced over at her. Her jaw was set, her arms stiff as she held the wheel, mentally preparing herself for the gory details that would hit all too close to home. "About the same as he did to you and Brian. Maybe a little more blood. She said Anatola mumbled, 'You aren't the right one, you're not Paige,' when he sliced at her." He didn't add that Jasmine had look bewildered when she added, "Since when would *I* want to be *Paige?*"

"At least she could talk," Paige said.

"She chatted up a storm when Brian arrived. I think she was more excited than terrified. Go figure."

Paige didn't respond and John tried not to

conjecture a reason for her silence, but he'd seen her face when she got her first glimpse of her former fiancé. He'd also seen the way she'd drooped when Brian's thoughts turned to Jasmine. John had known Paige only two days, but they'd been an intense two days. He knew her expressions.

"I'm not happy she was hurt," Paige said. "I wouldn't want you to think I was mean-hearted."

John laughed softly. "The last thing I think you are is mean-hearted." As he'd pressed a cloth on the worst of Jasmine's wounds, he'd had no option but to look at her. She'd obviously been nude under the sheet, and it had been impossible not to notice her breakneck curves.

She'd even managed to flirt with John until Brian showed up. John imagined Jasmine was not an easy woman for other women to care about but one most men would make a deal with the devil to possess.

"Did Jasmine tell you that Anatola took Brian's gun out of his bedside drawer?" Paige asked.

"Brian has a gun?"

"Brian *had* a gun. Now Anatola *has* a gun. And Brian and Katy and Jasmine will all be telling the police about this man. They'll find

his prints and match them with those in the Pollocks' car. The truth will start to unwind."

"I hope so," John said. "I wouldn't mind
knowing the truth."

She spared him a quick glance. As they approached Lone Tree, the traffic had picked up
and now they were traveling over a graceful
bridge toward the city itself. "So you haven't
remembered anything about your life?"

"Nothing."

"It must be extremely disconcerting."

"That's an understatement."

With one hand, she gestured at the stately
buildings rising around them. "I don't suppose
anything here strikes you as familiar."

John shook his head. "In a way it kind of
does."

"Really?"

"Don't get too excited. It seems familiar the
same way handling a gun and driving a car
seem familiar. My place in this piece of the
world isn't clear at all, though. I don't remember working here, I don't remember friends or
family, and worst of all, I don't remember where
I live...."

His voice trailed off when she hit her forehead with an open palm. "I'm an idiot," she said
under her breath. "I've just been too distracted
to think clearly."

She drove a little way farther before pulling to the curb in front of a motel. She switched off the engine and turned, searching the backseat for something.

"Why are you an idiot? Can I help you find something?"

"Where's my laptop?" she insisted.

"Right there under that coat. I'll get it for you."

He retrieved the computer for her and waited while she opened the case, bringing it to life.

"Just as I hoped," she said, typing quickly.

"What's just as you hoped?"

"We're picking up the motel's internet connection. I'm going to look you up on Google."

And as he watched, she did just that. The screen instantly filled with links to him and he looked away, not sure how to handle an onslaught of information that might reveal things about himself he didn't want to share with her.

No way around it, though.

"Mostly updates on the police search and your supposed victims, although there's mention here of another person being wanted for questioning. That's probably me or Anatola Korenev. Anyway, here's something about you personally. Want to know?"

"No," he said.

"John?"

"Okay. Just leave out the bad stuff."

"You're divorced," she informed him. "No children. Ex-police. John, you were a cop before you became a bodyguard. In fact, you were a hero. You pushed a congressman out of the way of an armed gunman last year. Hey, I remember reading about that. That was you?"

"You're asking me?"

"Sorry." She read for several seconds without speaking. John was beginning to get nervous when she said, "Well, anyway, you're thirty-nine years old and adopted, but it says not much is known about your early life. You work in Lone Tree as a bodyguard and are currently missing. They quote a woman named Natalie Dexter, who's identified as a friend of yours, as saying you left town three days ago on a job. And it gives your address."

"We can punch it into the GPS," John said.

She was typing again. "We don't have to. I found it on here. Looks like we passed the area where you live about three miles ago. It's on the other side of the bridge." She folded the computer shut and handed it to John.

As she made a U-turn and headed back the other way, John thought back to what they'd passed before getting on the bridge. The area had looked industrial to him, not residential, with train tracks running alongside the river and big warehouses sharing space with fenced, paved lots.

"Ready to go home?" Paige chirped as they started back across the bridge.

He nodded, filled with dread. It wasn't every day a man had to confront the unknown essence of his own life. He just hoped he hadn't buried any skeletons in plain view....

PAIGE COULDN'T GET THE passage she'd read about John—and hadn't related to him—out of her mind. As she drove the nearly vacant streets of what appeared to be the area of the city where shipping and receiving took place, she considered telling him the part she'd omitted.

But she couldn't believe it. John guilty of accepting a drug bribe? Everything she knew about him went against such a thought, and she did her best to shove it out of her head.

It wouldn't go far. She glanced at him now as he scanned the numbers on the buildings, not sure how he would take this kind of news about himself, because sooner or later she had to tell him. Keeping it to herself was the chicken's way out, but it seemed cruel to ambush him with more vague questions about his character.

The truth was if she couldn't reconcile this information with the man seated beside her, what was he supposed to make of it?

"How are we going to know Anatola Korenev isn't at your place waiting for us?" she asked.

"We're not. He could easily have been here by now."

"Or he could be one step behind us. I still don't understand why he went after me when he must have known how to get to you."

"Maybe he figures I'm too smart to go home until he's caught. Slow down. We're passing 31002 River Road. My building is 31006. Do you see an apartment house or something?"

Paige slowed way down. The place where John's house or condo or apartment should have perched was nothing more than a warehouse much like all the others, with a high metal fence surrounding it and an empty parking area in front. The gate was secured with a rusty-looking chain and a serious-looking lock about the size of a piece of sandwich bread. There was no sign announcing what the building held and there were no windows on the ground floor.

John whistled. "I live in a warehouse?"

"Next to Brown's Storage and Transfer and across the street from Lone Tree Moving," Paige said. "Your building is smaller than theirs."

"Maybe I rent a space here for my bodyguard business."

"Do bodyguards have offices?"

"Why are you asking me?" he snapped, and

then shook his head and smiled. "Sorry. I guess my nerves are getting to me. Well, I don't see an old black truck or a police car." He looked around again. "See that alley over there? It must wind around to the back of this place. I don't like sitting out here in plain view."

Paige drove down the dirt-and-rock-strewn alley, skirting receiving gates and Dumpsters. The back of John's place was as barren as the front, but there was an indentation and a door near the right corner of the building. Sliding metal doors large enough to drive a big truck through occupied space to their right. A row of dark windows appeared on what must be a second floor.

"There's no break in the fence," John said, "except the gate out front and this one. The front one had that cartoon-looking lock. I don't see any lock on this gate." He turned to face Paige. "This was as far as you signed on to go," he said.

"You want me to leave you three miles from town in back of a building you can't get into? No way."

"I'm going over, through or around that fence," he said.

"But the building will be locked."

"Probably. And I might trigger a silent alarm. Who knows? Anatola could be there already, waiting for me. But there's only one direction I can go at this point, and that's forward. So, you leave and I'll call you when I—"

"I'll wait here until you go reconnoiter," she said.

Much to her relief, he nodded. "At the first sign of trouble, please, look out for yourself. It's bad enough all these other people have suffered because of me. I couldn't stand it if you…"

There was one good way to shut him up, and Paige took it. She closed the distance between them and kissed him. The way his body stiffened announced he was stunned by her action, which amused her for a second, and then the fireworks started and she forgot to be amused.

They drew apart after a few seconds and stared at each other. He ran two fingers along her unhurt cheek in an incredibly longing manner. She took a shuddering breath as she gazed into his eyes.

Who was he? The kind, interesting, challenging John Cinca sitting so close right this moment, or a cohort of Anatola Korenev and a man who left the police department under a cloud of doubt about his honesty? And why was it so important to her to know the answer?

At the very least, this kiss had inched them away from the weirdness of the morning. This kiss was just a kiss—and yet a hint of so much more.

What about the way your heart leaped when Brian called you darling? You threw away everything he'd ever done to you in that one moment of bliss.

She was all over the map.

"Be careful," she finally murmured.

He kissed her one more time then let himself out of the car, leaving his bulky jacket and cowboy hat behind. He looked tall and powerful as he approached the fence. He stood there for a moment, then reached out and grabbed it and pulled on it as though testing it. With a sudden leap, he attached himself to the fence and began the laborious task of finding footholds and pulling himself to the top, where, crouching, he hovered a second before letting himself down by holding on to the top bar, extending his body on the other side and letting go. He landed six feet later, solidly, but it must have jarred him up to his teeth.

Half cat burglar, half cat.

Glancing back, he gave her a thumbs-up and then raced toward the building as though a gunman on the top floor had him in his sights. His condensed breath created a cloud around his head.

JOHN TOOK A DEEP BREATH as he hovered in the shallow doorway of the warehouse. The panel was metal, without windows, but there was a security camera mounted above it. A metal lever-type handle was connected to a tubular latch. There was no keyhole and no way to break inside.

He studied the apparatus for a few seconds. This was his door. Somewhere in his head he had to know how to open it.

Reaching out, he slid up the top part of the cover, revealing a bright blue sensor pad underneath. Without thinking, he touched the pad with his right pointer finger. The door beeped and clicked. He pushed down on the lever and it opened. The interior lights immediately flashed on, and what John saw left him speechless.

He glanced back at Paige's car before closing the door. The lights stayed on as though connected to a motion sensor.

The warehouse floor was occupied by a half dozen old fire trucks. There was also space for a vehicle of some kind, he assumed the one that had been abandoned in the park. There were two other vehicles already in their spaces, one a brand-new convertible and the other an SUV.

It was an unheated space and in the current conditions, freezing. He opened the brass door of a panel located directly to the right of the door and found several switches, many of which seemed to control outside lights and one that was marked Ground Floor Doors and another marked Gate.

Directly in front of him, a metal staircase led up to an encapsulated loft that occupied about half of the upper area. The area above where he stood disappeared into shadows high overhead.

He started up the stairs, mentally preparing himself for—well, for whatever. Who knew *what* was up here?

The stairs ended on a narrow landing. The door up here had been hacked to pieces. As John drew his gun and stepped inside, interior lights snapped on.

It looked to be more or less one large area, mostly open with a modest amount of decent furniture. The most impressive thing about the place was a baby grand piano near the windows. It also seemed to be about the only item that hadn't been tossed, dumped or overturned.

Papers and books and a million little things littered the floor. Furniture had been slashed. Obviously, someone had come looking for something while John was away. Had they found it?

How had they gotten past the door downstairs and the gate, for that matter?

He bypassed the curved bar that defined the kitchen, which was also a mess, then opened a door near the bedroom. That turned out to be a bathroom. The place was obviously deserted, so he put his gun away. Time to go get Paige.

He went back downstairs, shivering in the cold air, and pushed buttons, resulting in the soft hum of motors. He walked outside to the gate as it rolled open, and Paige met him.

"I think we should leave your car out here on this side of the fence," he said.

"But someone could see it," she said, shivering, her gaze traveling up and down the alley. "Someone like Korenev."

"Still, if we lock it inside the gates with us and something goes wrong—"

"Your call," she said.

"Someone has already been here looking for something," he said. "The place is torn apart."

She covered her mouth with two fingers. "Korenev was here. I completely forgot about it. He told me there was no trace of me at your place in Lone Tree."

"Well, from the look of things, he's worked his usual magic."

"Is there a dead body—"

"No, I didn't mean that. He just trashed the place."

She locked the car and they hurried across the yard together toward the warehouse. Through the open doors, John could see the glimmer of red paint and polished brass.

"How did you get inside without a key?" she asked him. "Wait, are those fire engines?"

"Yes. Neat, huh? And I got inside because it's a sensor lock that I obviously programmed. It reacted to my fingerprint. I wonder how Korenev got in."

As she walked into the warehouse, a low whistle escaped her lips. "Holy cow! Is this all yours?"

"I guess so," he said as he pushed the switch that closed the outside gate as well as the sliding doors and reactivated the interior lights. The place seemed to dazzle with all that machinery kept in pristine condition.

"It's cold in here," she said, looking around. The tremor was gone from her voice and he thought she was no doubt reacting to the sense of safety being behind closed, locked doors afforded. But it could be a false sense of security, and he was anxious to try to find something that made sense of this mess and then get out of here.

"It's a little warmer upstairs," he said.

"Wait a second," she said as he put a foot on the first metal stair. She walked between the engines, running her hand along their gleaming cherry surfaces, little *oohs* and *aahs* following her like a wake of ducklings trying to keep up with their mom. It pleased the hell out of him to hear her excited cries and see the gleam in her eyes as she scanned each vehicle. He wasn't sure why it pleased him. It just did.

"I've always loved fire engines," she said. She grinned. "I wonder if you have a dalmatian."

"I haven't seen one," he said. "What's your fascination with engines?"

"I told you, my father was a fireman. He used to let me sit in the engine and pretend to drive. I always thought I would be a fireman when I grew up, then I got interested in design and art. Still, there's just something about a fire truck. These look as though they belong in a museum. John, do you think the fact you collect fire engines and have obviously been in a fire sometime in your past are connected?"

A flame momentarily flared behind John's eyes as the mended skin over the old burns grew tight. *Something about a fire*...no, it was gone. He said, "I don't know. Seems possible."

"Yes." She paused in front of a very shiny red truck with an enclosed cab and an open back filled with hoses and tanks. There was a siren on the hood and a huge wench on the bumper. Lone Tree Vol. Fire Co. was printed in black and white on the door, along with the number 302.

"This one is absolutely charming," she said as she stepped up on the running board. "Look, the window is down and something is caught," she added as she grabbed the handle and pulled open the door.

Gasping, she pushed herself away from the truck as though poisonous snakes had jumped out to bite her. John scrambled to catch her before she hit the cement floor, then turning with her in his arms, peered into the cab to see what could have caused such a violent and spontaneous reaction.

With the opening of the door, a body had fallen toward them, face up, legs jammed under the wheel.

The man appeared elderly. He also appeared to be very, very dead.

Chapter Nine

"Who is that?" Paige gulped.

John shook his head as he set her on her feet. "I don't have the slightest idea."

She looked away, her stomach churning, her head reeling. Three dead bodies in two days was way too much to handle.

"I'm checking the other trucks," John said, and she could hear in his voice the dread that each might contain a body. She herself seemed unable to move except to turn her head.

But not staring at the man did not obliterate the image that was stuck in her mind. He looked elderly, over eighty, with white hair and wire-framed glasses that had been knocked awry. There was a slash across his throat, but he was dressed in dark clothes so it wasn't easy to see blood....

Her stomach rolled and she closed her eyes, holding on to the wall for support. All around her, she heard doors opening and slamming shut as John checked for more bodies.

She was aware of his return when he put his hands on her shoulders and turned her to face him. "No more dead people," he said. "The poor old guy must have been killed right there in the truck. It's so cold decay was slowed down."

"I wonder how Korenev got that close to him."

"I wonder." John closed his eyes as he took a deep breath and then fixed his gaze on her face. "I sure as hell hope I didn't help kill this guy."

"Of course you didn't," Paige said. "We should check the body for some sort of identification."

"Like a wallet? I don't think so. It's unlikely his name would mean anything to either of us, and I don't want to make an official investigation any harder than it's going to be already."

"Spoken like a policeman."

"Spoken like a man who doesn't want any of his DNA on a dead body." He ran his free hand through his hair. "I wonder if he's a relative of mine. How creepy is that? I could be looking at my own father's body and not even know it." He swore to himself and studied his feet for a moment. Frustration was written all over the handsome angles and planes of his face.

"You were adopted," she reminded him, un-

sure how that could help. Adopted father or natural one, uncle or stranger, the result was the
same. A man was dead, murdered in John's own
space. And John didn't know for sure whom he
was or how he got there.

Nerves and fear scratched at her skin, and
suddenly her mind was filled with fear for everyone she knew or cared for. "I have to call
Katy."

"Her phone is dead, remember?"

"Oh, yeah. Well, I'll call Matt."

She made the call to Matt's cell and he picked
up on the first ring. In the background, Paige
heard what sounded like a game on television
and the sound of other voices. Male voices.

"Are you guys almost done?" she asked.

Matt had to talk loud to be heard. "We're
getting there. Oh, and Katy says to tell you she
called the cops and gave a description of Brian's
uncle and told them you were okay and all and
you should stop worrying."

"You tell her I'll stop worrying when she gets
the hell out of that apartment," Paige said and
hung up, looking around the warehouse, looking anywhere but at the poor, dead man spilling out of the truck. There simply was no good
way to put his body back to how it had been.

The place felt like a morgue, and she shiv-
ered, anxious to get out of here.

"Don't you wonder why I have so much security?" John said.

She turned her attention to him. Was it possible his disgrace with the police department and his lifestyle were connected? She had to tell him about his past.

Before she could, he seemed to shake off his doubts. "I'm going upstairs to see if I can find out something about myself. Good, bad or indifferent, I have to know." He gestured at the convertible and the SUV. "I obviously have transportation now, so you're free—"

"To return to my apartment where Anatola Korenev has already made a cameo appearance? Oh, wait, what apartment? Sister dearest is cleaning it out even as we speak. Or I could knock on Brian's door and ask where he dumped all my belongings. Nope, I'm staying with you until this is resolved. Don't ask me why, but I feel safe with you, so just get used to me."

He smiled that way he had that seemed to say so much with so little effort. "I shouldn't admit it but I'm glad. Let's look around upstairs."

"And I need to wash up," she said.

She didn't take in many details as she made her way through the clutter to the bathroom, which seemed to sport the only real walls in the place. She ran warm water over her hands and scrubbed every inch of exposed skin with soap as though she could wash away evil. It took a while.

Stomach still in a knot, she rejoined John, finding he'd uprighted a chair and was sitting at his desk. There was a roomy satchel at his feet containing what appeared to be a few pieces of clothing and a box of ammunition.

When he saw the direction of her gaze, he explained. "Might as well be prepared, right? I grabbed some stuff."

"Smart thinking."

The desk was situated against an outside wall on which were mounted three black-and-white video monitors, two of which appeared to be working. The other had been smashed. The monitor on the far wall showed the front of the warehouse, the one next to it, the back door.

"Find anything in the desk?" she asked, glancing out the window at the empty yard below. No sign of the police…yet.

"I picked a few pictures up off the floor," he said, gesturing at a small pile.

"Any sign of a computer?"

"None. Whoever did this must have taken it. I found a cord, but the machine is gone."

As John continued searching the desk, running his hands inside the drawer cavity and under the top, Paige studied the photographs.

In one John wore a mortarboard and held a diploma—looked like a college graduation. In another it appeared he was graduating from the police academy. There was one of him taken with a very pretty redhead with a ski lift backdrop signed *Love: Natalie* across one corner and another with a shorter, swarthier man who held in his arms a tiny girl with huge brown eyes. And there was one taken of a polished antique fire engine in the middle of a parade of some sort.

She showed the picture of the redhead to John. "Ring any bells?"

He'd been knocking on the front panels of the old wood desk, but he paused to look at the picture. "Nope."

"How about this?" she said, handing him the photo of the fire engine. "Is that one of the rigs downstairs?"

"I don't know. It could be the big one in the back. Wait a second." He plucked a magnifier from the mess at his feet and angled it over the photo. "I think that's me standing on the running board. Hey, take a look at the driver."

He showed the photo to Paige, who squinted as she peered through the glass. "He looks like the guy downstairs."

John turned the photo over. "No names. It's dated three years ago, though."

Paige went back to the stack and shuffled through a few of what appeared to be vacation shots taken in Hawaii. "Any of these jar any memories?" she asked.

"None. Wait a second, this is a false front. Listen when I knock." He rapped his fingers against the desk panel...it did sound hollow. Running his hands over the wood, he finally managed to slide open a small hidden compartment.

From this, he withdrew a manila envelope, and they both cleared off room on the desktop. John emptied the contents. "My passport," he said. "And another photo."

In this picture, a young teenage version of John stood between a man and woman who looked way too old to be his parents. Behind them she could see a river and one end of a bridge with green turrets. It looked somehow familiar to Paige.

She had checked the reverse side of every photo for identifying names or locations and found very little. This time she struck gold in the form of names. *Sergi, John and Galina Ogneva, 1988* was written in block letters.

"Eureka," John said.

She glanced at him but he wasn't looking at the photo; his attention was focused on the passport. He opened it and perused the pages. "Late last year, I went to Canada," he said. "A few months later, I flew to Kanistan."

"Kanistan," Paige repeated. "That's in the Ukraine somewhere, isn't it?"

"Yes."

"Wait a second, I remember," she said, tapping the top photograph with a fingertip. "Look at this picture. See that turret? It's an unusual color and shape. It's on a bridge that crosses over to a big hotel that sits on an island in the middle of a lake. It looks like a fairy-tale castle in the winter when the lake freezes over and everything is covered with ice. I used an image of it in a calendar a few years ago."

He studied the photograph, his finger touching the people. "Who are they?"

"The adults are Sergi and Galina Ogneva and the kid is you."

He flipped the photo over and then back again. "So, where is this place?"

"Kanistan."

"Anatola Korenev's accent sounds eastern European, doesn't it?" John said.

"It sure does." They needed more information. She began to pick through the remaining papers when she realized John's attention was now riveted on one of the outside monitors.

An old, dented, heavy-duty van with an oversize grille and enough antennae to track a satellite had pulled up to the front gate. As they watched, the door opened and a man with a bushy black beard got out of the car. He wore a bandage on his right hand. As he approached the fence and shook the chain and lock, Paige's stomach did a belly flop.

"That's Korenev," she mumbled.

John swore. "He's getting back in the van. Maybe he's leaving."

Indeed, the old vehicle backed up thirty feet, but then shot forward toward the gate. The crash was silent to them, but the monitor screen filled with the images of flying metal as the van battered half of it away.

"Quick, get everything back in the envelope," John said, scooping up the passport and the other papers.

Paige stuffed the photos in her pockets. She glanced up at the monitors to see Korenev at the back door now, holding a huge gun that looked as if it belonged in a war zone. He fired at the door. The sound traveled up the stairs into the loft. The screen filled with smoke. They'd be sitting ducks if they attempted to use the stairs.

From below, they heard gunfire, then Korenev's booming voice. "I see you found old man," he yelled. "You two go next to join him. No mercy this time."

No mercy this time? Was the man delusional?

Since when had he ever shown anyone any mercy?

A bullet shattered one of the glass panels, and Paige retreated deeper into the room as glass rained down on the floor. My God, they were trapped. They were going to die. Korenev wasn't fooling around with knives. He had himself an honest-to-goodness automatic weapon and there was nowhere to go....

John grabbed her hand and pulled her into the kitchen, where they hunkered down near the floor, in among cooking gear and dishcloths. He fired off a shot toward the open doorway, which was around the corner from them. "There has to be a fire escape," he said.

"I didn't see anything under any of the windows—"

"We couldn't see the northeast side from any of our positions. It has to be over there." He fired off another round. "Go find it and use it. Once you're outside, you'll have to go out the front gate and run back to your car."

"What about you?"

"I'll try to slow him down. Go."

"You'll follow?"

"If I can," he said, pushing her away.

"John..."

"Please," he said, with a hasty look. "Go."

As he fired again, she scooted out of the

kitchen and made her way back to the northeast corner. Out of the corners of her eyes, she saw John creep toward the shattered interior window. The sound of ammunition firing underscored urgency, but leaving him to face Korenev alone was the hardest thing she'd ever done.

Okay, a fire escape had to be attached outside the windows in either the bedroom or the bathroom. Those were the only areas in that corner and she hadn't seen anything when she was in the bathroom. Maybe it was a rope piled inside a closed drapery, though. She'd have to look. She flew around the big bed, stumbling when she hit a stool, knocking it aside and catching herself by grabbing for a bedpost. She tore open the drapery covering the bedroom window.

And there it was, a metal platform affixed to the outside of the window with an attached ladder. She opened the window and screamed at John as she picked up a stray boot and popped out the screen. She followed it out onto the fire escape.

The platform sported a railing on one side and felt steady enough under her feet, but it appeared the ladder was cantilevered. As she put her weight on it, it creaked and groaned and began to descend. She grabbed for the hand railing and for a dizzying moment thought she was going to fall.

Holding on for dear life, she proceeded down the ladder, trusting it would support her and praying John would find a way to follow.

JOHN HEARD THE CLATTER of metal and hoped it meant Paige had found a way out of this hell-hole. Now he had to figure out how to stop Korenev.

From the direction of the shots, he knew Korenev was on the stairs but he dared not risk looking for an exact location. He could if he had a mirror, however, but where did a guy like him keep a mirror in a place like this except fastened to a medicine cabinet? There wasn't time to fool with that.

Wait a second. He was right next to the kitchen, and he must be some kind of gourmet cook because he'd spied a whole rack covered with stainless-steel pans.

He covered his movements with more shots and took one of the frying-pan lids from the rack. The top of the lid, the side without the handle, was very reflective. Holding it like a shield, he got back in position by the broken window.

"Here goes nothing," he muttered, inching the lid above his head with one hand while firing the gun with the other as a distraction. Korenev returned fire and by angling the shiny lid and happening onto a wayward shaft of light, John was able to pinpoint Korenev's position.

Korenev was halfway up the stairs, creeping closer. The weapon he toted was not the gun he'd lifted from Brian Witherspoon—this was an assault weapon that would tear a man's flesh off his bones.

A second later, Korenev must have spied the makeshift mirror because he fired a shot. John released the lid just in time to keep from losing a finger or two. In the next instant, he stood and fired. A roar from Korenev thundered on the stairs. A second later, the big man fell to the cement floor, and it seemed the building shook. John risked a look.

Korenev had survived the fall. He was grasping his left leg, but he was already repositioning his weapon…. The guy was like a cockroach—invincible.

Time to get out of there. John ran across the apartment as fast as anyone could. He was on the fire escape and down to the ground without even noticing he'd grabbed his satchel in passing. There was no sign of Paige. He debated going to the back and shooting out the van tires, but that would put him in direct sight of the door.

He heard an engine behind him and turned to see Paige's car. She pulled to a stop beside him and he yanked open the door and fell into the passenger seat.

"Where's Korenev?" she asked.

"I wounded him. Go back down that alley."

"Is he going to follow us?"

"Not if I take out a tire or two."

Korenev had figured out how to open the sliding doors and stood inside, stooped over, but he straightened when he heard the advancing car. The van was too far away for a debilitating hit from John's revolver, and no way did he want to drive into that yard and get close to a madman wielding an AK-47. He took a shot at Korenev for good measure…and missed. Korenev raised his weapon.

"Let's get out of here," John yelled.

Paige pressed down on the accelerator and they shot toward the street.

John turned in the seat to watch the road behind them. So far, so good.

"Now we know for sure Korenev killed the man in the fire truck," Paige said, "and that you didn't have anything to do with it."

"Yeah. I think the old man must have been at my place taking care of the fire trucks or something when Korenev showed up. Maybe the old guy left the gate open and the sliding doors, too. Maybe Korenev just rolled right in, walked up to the open window and overpowered him. Then he went upstairs and took what he wanted."

"I wonder what he wanted," she said.

"I do, too."

"And if he just steals whatever he wants, including cars, why does he keep taking old wrecks?"

"Probably because they're easier to hot-wire. And maybe it has something to do with the fact their owners might make less of a fuss when their vehicle turns up missing."

Once again, they flew over the bridge into the city. John held on for dear life as Paige took a sudden right, and then they were traveling downhill into the dark.

He turned in the seat to find she'd entered a parking garage. She pulled up to the automated gate and took a ticket. The arm swung up and she steered them to the ramp that led up, and then kept going until they were on the roof. She parked in the southwest corner, where they could see the entrance of the garage three stories below.

"What now?" she asked as she turned to him. She dug his photos out of her pockets as though just remembering them. Most were creased, one was torn.

He took them from her and looked through them, studying each, hoping something would awaken some little memory that would leap-frog into total recollection. He paused when he got to the one of him as a child. That it was him there could be little doubt. Same shoulders, same eyes, same ears.

"Nothing is helping me get my memory back," he said, discouraged almost to the breaking point. What was it going to take?

Paige took the manila envelope out of the satchel and reached inside for the passport. "You didn't travel a whole lot before the Canadian trip and then the one to Kanistan last month. And you went one day and came home the next."

"I wonder why I went."

"This looks like an address book," she said, liberating a small, red leather-bound book. "See if any of the names jump out at you."

She stared at him as he searched the pages, her eyes anxious, her fingers pleating the hem of her jacket. He had one of those funny feelings that she was trying to find a way to tell him something. "What's on your mind?" he asked.

Her eyelashes fluttered against her cheeks. She cleared her throat. "There's something I didn't mention. Something about you."

"Great." He heaved a deep breath. "Okay, I'm ready. What is it?"

"You're not going to like it, so I'm just going to spit out the facts because that's all I know, anyway. The reason you left the police department was because you got caught accepting a drug bribe. It didn't say how much or anything. I guess the department kind of settled for you paying back the money and leaving quietly because of your hero status thanks to saving the congressman. I'm sorry I held it back."

He was a cheat, too? In addition to what else? And if he'd been drummed out of the very department that was undoubtedly now looking for him, would he even have a chance to plead his case before they locked him away?

How did you defend your character when you didn't know what kind of character you had, especially when there was a dead guy in your place of residence?

"I don't know what to make of that information right now," he said at last. "I'm going to try to ignore it for the time being." He studied the names on the page: Addison, Burton, Carlisle. No bells, no whistles, no nothing. Not until he hit the *D*s. "Here's something."

"Someone you remember?" Paige asked anxiously.

"No. But I've seen the first name recently. Natalie, last name Dexter. Isn't she the redhead in the photo?"

"Yes, yes." Paige shuffled through the photos and handed him the right one. "This might be her or it might not be. The woman who gave the interview was named Natalie, too, and she must have known you pretty well. It's got to be the same person. I'm going to talk to her." Paige drew out her cell phone. "Give me her number."

He read it off as she punched in numbers.

Paige waited a moment or two and then said, "Natalie? Natalie Dexter? Yes, hello, my name is, uh, Julia. Julia Roberts." She laughed and added, "No, not the movie star, I'm afraid. Actually, I'm a writer doing a story on John Cinca for a newspaper. Oh, just a little one up in the mountains. I was wondering if I could ask you a few questions."

She listened for a bit. John tried to read what was going on, but for once her expression was neutral. She shook her head as she resumed speaking. "Well, actually, I'm not in the mountains right now. I'm in Lone Tree because of a family thing. I saw your name on a report." Another pause to listen followed by a sucked-in breath of excitement. "You will? Right now? I'm sure I can find it. I'll meet you there in twenty minutes. Thank you."

"You warned me you were a good liar," John said when she hung up.

"Nice of you to notice," she said.

"Except for the Julia Roberts thing."

"I drew a blank." She returned his flicker of

a smile, then turned serious again. "I need to find Sunshine Coffeehouse. She said it was on Main." Paige gestured toward the street below. "That's Main down there."

"I'll go," he said.

"No, you won't. Who knows how this woman feels about you? One glance and she might call the police. Besides, you live and work here. Your face was all over the place when you saved that congressman. Anyone might recognize you. This place can't be too far away. Natalie gave me a cross street and I remember seeing it when we first drove into town. Vine, that's it. Main and Vine. I'll go meet her and come back here and we'll figure out the next step. Stay out of sight, okay?"

He wanted to protest, he wanted to take control—this was his life even if it currently resembled an avalanche.

But she made sense. He would stay in the car and look at every scrap of paper they'd salvaged and maybe something would get through to his subconscious.

"Now it's my turn to tell you to be careful," he said. "Anatola Korenev knows exactly what you look like."

"You shot him. His leg was all bloody."

"You don't really think a little thing like that will stop him?" John said.

PAIGE RECOGNIZED THE woman from the photograph the moment she walked into the crowded coffeehouse. Though seated, Natalie Dexter appeared tall and willowy with large, green, expressive eyes framed by waves of auburn hair. She wore a faux-fur-collared sweater over trim slacks and sipped something frothy from a coffee mug.

"Natalie?" Paige said in greeting.

Natalie gave Paige a quick once-over and smiled. "You must be Julia," Natalie said, extending a hand. She gestured at her coffee and added, "Would you like something?"

"What you're having looks great. I'll go up to the counter—"

"No need, sit, please, the waiter here is really nice." Natalie waved a hand and a young man in an apron appeared at her side as though he'd been awaiting her summons. "Will you bring us another nonfat mocha, Billy?" she asked.

The coffee arrived as Paige draped her coat over the back of her chair. She'd stopped at a drugstore along the way and bought an inexpensive digital audio recorder. She dug that out of her handbag and said, "Do you mind?"

"I guess not," Natalie said. "Like I mentioned on the phone, I'm a little pressed for time." She raised her left hand to glance at her watch. A large solitary diamond sparkled on her ring finger. It looked a whole lot like an engagement ring. "What would you like to ask me?"

Are you engaged to John Cinca? was what Paige wanted to ask, but she didn't. "How do you know Mr. Cinca?"

"We met when he was a policeman and I worked as a court stenographer," she said easily. "We started dating." She shrugged. "We got real close, even talked about marriage."

"But you didn't?"

"No." She sat back in her chair and met Paige's gaze. "Have you met John?"

Paige mentally crossed her fingers and lied. "No."

"He's a wonderful guy. I was crazy about him."

"But…?"

"But he had all these closed doors."

Paige took a drink of the warm, chocolate coffee to give herself a moment to think. It tasted comforting and homey, sensations that seemed almost foreign at this point.

"Could you explain what you mean by closed doors?" she asked.

"Oh, you know. Emotionally, he wasn't very available. It's not hard to understand why. I mean, he didn't know anything about himself before the age of ten because of the amnesia."

Paige clasped her hands together in her lap as she leaned forward. *"Amnesia?"*

Natalie glanced down at the tape recorder and shook her head. "I shouldn't have said that, especially to a reporter."

"I won't use it, I promise."

"Oh, come on."

"Please," Paige insisted. "You have to explain." Was it possible John's whole life was a blur?

"I can't. You'll print what I say in your newspaper."

"I won't, but even if I did, his life isn't a secret, is it?"

"He's very private."

"If he's suspected of murdering at least two people, do you really think his secrets will stay buried?"

Natalie bit her lip and shook her head.

Paige regarded the other woman with curiosity. "Why did you agree to talk to me if you didn't want to be honest about John? What's the point?"

Natalie's lips parted, then she shook her head again. "I'm worried about him, that's all. I hate hearing people talk about him like he's a monster. Whatever happened to innocent until proven guilty?" She looked away and then back. "I guess you're right. No matter what's going on, his life will be an open book from now on, won't it?"

"I think so," Paige said.

"He just didn't like to talk about the past because so much of it was unknown or unpleasant. John was an only child. When he was ten or so, he was in a car accident that killed his folks. He was in a coma for weeks. When he finally awoke, he didn't remember anything. Not his parents, not the accident, nothing. His grandparents explained everything, but there were big holes, missing details they refused to discuss. The grandparents told him his father had been American, working in England when he and John's mother, their estranged daughter, died. They showed him all his papers and everything, but they didn't speak much English. His teenage years were difficult, to say the least."

John was raised in Kanistan. Why didn't that surprise Paige? "I've heard he has burn scars," she said. "A result of the accident?"

"Apparently."

"I've also heard he collects antique fire engines."

"Oh, that. That's a new passion, but most of the collection actually belongs to a guy named Frank Elton, a strange old guy, kind of a hermit. I haven't seen John's new place in the warehouse district, but my fiancé has and he says it's full of fire trucks. He thinks John was allowing Mr. Elton to keep them there when he lost the lease on his old place. John always had a weak spot for both loners and firefighting equipment."

Frank Elton must be the dead man in the fire truck. Paige rubbed her neck as she pondered what to ask next. Her fingers rolled over the fine chain that supported the owl pendant. "Do you know anything about any, um, phobias, he might have?"

"Phobias? Like what?"

"Oh, you know, fear of snakes or bats or spiders or maybe owls?"

"No," Natalie said, brow furrowing.

"How about nightmares?"

"Some, but don't we all? These are odd questions."

Paige half smiled as her mind raced. Did this mean these dreams and this paranoia were recent manifestations? She realized Natalie was waiting for her to comment. "Oh, you know, just mining for tidbits," she said. "So how did Cinca end up back in the United States?"

"He ran away from Kanistan when he was seventeen. He said as soon as he got here he felt he'd finally come home."

"Did he have any family living stateside?"

"No. He never even sees his grandparents. I'm not sure they're still alive. He was married right out of college, but it didn't work out. John's about as alone as a man can get. But he's also a good man, Ms. Roberts."

"So you don't think he killed the Pollocks?"

Natalie shook her head. "I can't believe he did."

"You mentioned in the interview I read that Mr. Cinca took a job right before all this happened."

"Yes," Natalie said, obviously relieved to move away from discussing John's past. She lifted the mug of coffee to her lips, but set it back down without taking a sip and ran a finger around the lip.

"What are you thinking?" Paige asked softly.

Natalie met Paige's gaze. "Several months ago, right before the whole scandal with the bribery stuff, John told me he was going to Canada to see someone claiming to be a relative. Apparently this woman contacted him after seeing his picture in the paper when he saved Congressman Richards from that crackpot. When he got back, Kevin asked him how it went, and he wouldn't talk about it. The next thing I knew, he was headed to Kanistan."

"You know about Kanistan?"

"Of course. Even though we stopped dating, we stayed friends. In fact, he introduced me to my fiancé. Kevin is a policeman, too."

"But John isn't. He left the force because he took a bribe."

"He didn't take a bribe."

"The article I read said he pled guilty."

Natalie shook her head. "He didn't take a bribe," she repeated.

"How do you know?"

"I just know. And this time I am not explaining," she added with a pointed glance at the recorder. "I've already said too much as it is."

"The article was vague, too."

"They claimed he took money to look the other way. What other details do you want?"

"And he confessed," Paige repeated.

Natalie shrugged.

"Okay. Well, can you tell me who John went to Kanistan to see?"

Natalie suddenly turned coy. "Maybe he went on a vacation."

"For two days?" Paige said.

Natalie's eyebrows inched up her forehead. "You seem to know an awful lot about that trip."

Paige spoke the truth. "Actually, I don't know anything besides when he left and when he came back. I don't know why he went."

"Well, I don't, either."

Drat. "Do you know who his new client was?"

Natalie checked her watch, then opened her

purse and took out her wallet. She waved away Paige's offer to pay.

"No," she said, smiling at the waiter, who came to collect the money. "John came back from his Kanistan trip more tight-lipped than ever before, and that's saying something. I only know about the new client because Kevin and I invited John on a double date and he said he was going to be out of town, that he was acting as a bodyguard for some guy."

Paige sat back in her chair, thinking. She knew time was running out. "Recently I ran across a photograph of John standing next to a shorter, more burly looking guy holding a baby with beautiful brown eyes. Do you know who that is?"

"I guess it could be anybody, although it sounds a lot like his old partner on the force, Andy Patter. He and his wife adopted their little girl last year."

"Do you think Andy would be willing to talk to me?"

"Probably, but I'm not sure where he is. They moved away, and as far as I know no one has heard much from them."

"You mentioned a double date. Does that mean John was seeing someone new?"

"No, it means Kevin's cousin was visiting from out of town and we needed a date for her.

She and John had met and gotten along on her last visit, so naturally we thought of him." Natalie folded her napkin and set it beside her cup, then checked her watch again. "I'm meeting Kevin so I really have to go."

Paige stood at the same time. "Is there anything else you can tell me about John Cinca that will help my, uh, readers understand him better?"

Natalie paused as she buttoned her coat. "I can't think of anything." She gestured at the recorder. "On second thought, would you be willing to turn that off?"

"Sure." Paige flipped the on/off button and dropped the recorder in her pocket.

"I'm going to tell you something off the record," Natalie said, her voice softer than before. "Kevin heard the police found fingerprints from an unidentified person in the dead couple's home and in their car as well as on an old stolen truck abandoned at a little airstrip in the mountains somewhere."

"Prints coming from the same person?"

"Exactly. They're looking for this person but not announcing it. I don't think they really suspect John. I think they figure they'll run across his body, another victim of the real murderer. They're waiting for the man who was beaten up to regain consciousness and explain what happened to him." Natalie's eyes watered as she continued. "When you write this story, be careful what you say about John and how you say it, Ms. Roberts. If it turns out he's an innocent victim, your words could come back to haunt you."

Chapter Ten

Paige arrived back at the car a little pink from the cold, a little out of breath and carrying a bag from which issued the best aroma John had ever encountered. At least as far as he knew.

"What is that?" he asked as pure, unadulterated hunger drove both anxiety and curiosity away.

"Soup," she said.

John unpacked insulated containers of soup and packages of crackers while Paige settled behind the wheel. He handed her a cup and popped the lid off his own. "What kind is it?"

"Tomato basil bisque. It's all they had left."

"It's good," he said, taking a cautious sip from a plastic spoon. It was hot. Hot was good.

She produced a little recorder, which she placed on the dashboard.

"Don't tell me you taped your conversation with Natalie."

"Isn't that what an aspiring journalist does?" she asked with a smile. "Eat up while we listen."

Natalie Dexter had a nice voice but it sparked no memories. Obviously they'd been close and had remained friendly even though she'd moved on with her life. He tried to put some meaning to the name Kevin but drew yet another blank. He was sick of blanks.

He lost his appetite as he heard himself described as a man with closed doors. He felt naked sitting there in front of Paige, discussed and dissected by someone he couldn't remember knowing. And oddly enough, the compliments were just as embarrassing as the hesitations.

The silence after the tape finished made everything more difficult. John cleared his throat and took a deep breath. "So the dead man at my place is probably Frank Elton."

"Probably. And you were doing him a favor by allowing him to keep his collection at your place."

"Some favor. If he hadn't been there— Well, talk about water under the bridge. Why did Natalie want you to turn off the recorder?"

"Because she told me that Kevin had heard about the existence of a third man, one whose fingerprints were in the Pollocks' car and in a truck abandoned at a small airstrip."

"Anatola Korenev. So, that's how he got off

the mountain. That's why he was in a hurry. Somehow he'd arranged to have a plane waiting at that little airport."

"She also thinks you might be a victim yourself and warned me to be careful about what I wrote about you."

"It's kind of reassuring that she doesn't think I killed anyone. I mean, she knows me."

Paige touched his hand. "So do I."

"Okay, this is weird, but it never occurred to me that I should assure anyone I'm okay, that anyone would care one way or another. Isn't that odd?"

"I don't know, John. Given that you apparently suffered from amnesia after that accident when you were a kid—"

"And how about that? I've had amnesia twice in a lifetime? Doesn't that strike you as a little weird?"

"A little," Paige said, licking the last of the thick red soup off her spoon. John was momentarily distracted by the sight of her tongue sliding against her lips. *Less digging in the past, more wallowing in the present,* that's what his brain kept screaming at him. Or maybe it wasn't his *brain* sending that message.

Whoever, whatever, take her in your arms, scatter soup containers and crackers from the hood ornament to the trunk, make love like a crazy man. Use her to stay sane.

"I should have asked Natalie about your ex-wife," Paige said out of the blue. "I have her cell-phone number—I'm going to call her."

Paige made the call, spoke for a few minutes, then hung up.

"Well?" he asked. He'd been unable to get a feeling for the conversation by listening to Paige's end of it.

"You married a woman about two weeks after you met her. She said you haven't been in touch with her since the divorce over ten years ago. It didn't really sound like you discussed her much with Natalie."

"Another one of my damn closed doors," he muttered. He took a deep breath as Paige piled the garbage back into the bag. "I hate to tell you this," he added, "because I really like the way you keep thinking I'm a good guy, but Natalie may be wrong about my not taking bribes." He thumbed through the papers he'd found in the envelope and extracted the one he was looking for. "According to this bank statement, I deposited a hefty piece of change in a bank account late last year."

She glanced up. "How much?"

"Just over two million dollars."

"Yikes."

"And that was just in one account. In another, I deposited a million and have been steadily drawing from it. And there are other accounts— I must have been crooked for years."

"And stupid enough to put the money in the bank? That doesn't make sense." She took the paper from him and looked at the amounts and dates. "These deposits occurred after your trip to Canada. Natalie said you went to see a woman claiming to be a relative who sent you a note about having important information of a personal nature. You got back from Canada, left the police force, suddenly had a lot of money. John, we have to go to Canada. We have to try to figure out who you went to see and why, except how do we do that?"

"Carol Ann Oates," he said, and started digging through the papers again.

"Who's Carol Ann Oates?"

"A woman who lives in Deep Falls, Alberta, Canada. She sent me a letter last year." He found what he was looking for and read aloud. "'Dear John, I don't know how much you remember of me or the rest of your family. But I have important information you must know about. Come see me as quickly as you can. Carol Ann Oates.' There's a contact phone number."

"If this woman can tell you why you contacted her, we may start to understand some of this."

"My thoughts exactly. Do you want to call or should I?"

"You call. Let me look at that letter."

He placed the call. It took several rings, which even he knew was odd as almost everyone seemed to have answering machines and call waiting, but right before he was about to give up, a woman finally answered. He asked to speak to Carol Ann Oates.

The woman responded in such a thick French accent, John couldn't grasp a single word. "English?" he asked hopefully, and then uttered a resigned, "Please, slow down."

Paige touched his leg. "What's wrong?" she mouthed.

He covered the speaker. "I can't understand her. Thick French accent."

Paige extended a hand and he gave her the phone, his eyebrows rising as she began to speak.

"Quel est votre nom, s'il vous plaît?" she said.

After a moment, she continued. *"Bonjour, Gaelle. Puis-je parler à Madame Carol Ann Oates, s'il vous plaît?"*

She fell silent as Gaelle apparently spoke on the other end. Paige asked a few more questions, muttered, *"Merci, Mademoiselle Batiste,"* and hung up.

"You are full of surprises," John said.

"I speak Spanish, too, not that anyone can understand me. Gaelle Batiste is apparently a house sitter. She said she would have never divulged Madame Oates's location to a male, but it was okay to tell a woman. She recently traveled to a hospital in Montana specializing in alternative treatments."

"For what?"

"She didn't say. I gather she's very ill."

"And she's in Montana?"

"We have to go see her."

He thought for a moment—really, he was tired and gritty and so was she. But there wasn't any other option, he knew that. If they stood still too long, Korenev or the police would catch up with them. If there was a chance the Oates woman could clear things up so he could go to the police and get himself and, more important, Paige, out of danger, then he had to try.

"While you drive, I'll use the GPS and figure out a route," he said. "Where in Montana?"

"Up in the mountains near Seeley Lake at a place called Deer Creek Spa."

They left Lone Tree as the sun set over the bridge.

PAIGE MADE IT UNTIL about 7:00 p.m. before John took over driving. They listened to the news every hour, hoping to hear Anatola Korenev had been apprehended, but the only update concerned news of a new unnamed suspect. Nothing of the attack at Brian's apartment or the mess at John's warehouse home were mentioned.

At midnight, Paige woke up with a jolt as it registered in her subconscious they were no longer moving. She opened her eyes to find herself staring at an illuminated sign that said Lamp Light Motel. A smaller vacancy sign shone like the promise of paradise.

"I can't go any further," John said, suppressing a yawn with his fist. "My eyes can't focus. I'm a danger on the highway."

"I can't, either," Paige admitted. "I'll go see if they have a room."

"Just one," he said, holding up a finger. "Anatola is out there somewhere. I think we should stay together."

She hesitated, remembering the way John had woken up that morning.

He mistook her silence. "Don't be offended but I am entirely too tired to threaten your virtue," he said. "Not that I wouldn't love to have a go at it another time."

She laughed as she got out of the car, but the

worry of what the morning would bring didn't strike her as very funny.

It was obvious the bearded man who appeared out of the back room when Paige hit the bell on the desk had been asleep. He appeared disinterested in anything, including license-plate numbers and names. As Paige had taken money out of an ATM after seeing Natalie, she paid in cash. The bearded man handed her a key, warned her the vibrating bed was broken and staggered off to the back room before Paige could get out of the tiny lobby.

There were exactly two cars in the almost-empty parking lot. At John's suggestion, they pulled around to the back of the building and tucked the car close to the probable bathroom window of their ground-floor unit.

The room turned out to be narrow and small but amazingly clean. Paige took the first shower, scrubbing her skin and hair until she felt brand new again, doing her best to put thoughts of John aside. But when she pulled on the same nightclothes she'd worn the first time they met—in her bed, no less—she had to admit he was never far from her mind.

He looked her over when she entered the room. He'd been watching TV and he switched it off. The way he looked at her made her afraid and anxious and terribly aware of him, all at the same time.

"What are you looking at?" she asked, her voice soft.

"Short answer? You."

"Dare I ask the long answer?"

He turned off the television, smiling. "Well, I believe I may have discovered something new about myself."

"A memory?"

"More like a suspicion. I think I may have spent my life as a leg man. And don't get me wrong, you have a great set of legs. But seeing you in a T-shirt that clings to your body that way, well, I may actually be a breast guy."

She laughed. "Thank you. I think."

"You're welcome."

She gestured at the television. "Did you make the news?"

"Flooding in the south and a sniper attack in D.C. have pushed most regional stuff off the screen," he said. "There were some interesting things, though." Instead of telling her what they were, he caught her hand. "You sure tidy up nice, Ms. Graham."

"Thank you," she said. "It feels wonderful to be clean."

"I'll know in a minute when I take mine. Hell, we should have shared one and saved the water."

She smiled. "Tell me about the news."

"They still haven't revealed Korenev's name. I'm betting he's using an alias, but a guy like that has to have prints on file somewhere. Oh, and the victim from the park is still unconscious. They also mentioned the woman identified as Paige Witherspoon in earlier reports is actually Paige Graham and has turned up safe and accounted for."

"Well, accounted for anyway. Maybe now we should go to the cops—"

"No. Not yet. I can't. Don't ask me to."

She nodded.

He took the next shower while Paige towel-dried her fine hair and spent a few minutes checking out the quick mend of her necklace with the meager tools of her cosmetic bag. The necklace John couldn't bring himself to even touch....

How could she be attracted to a man when she knew he was known for being emotionally unavailable? That's what Natalie had said, and she'd said it with regret. She didn't strike Paige as a fickle woman. And Paige had a track record of falling for good-looking guys in the midst of their most vulnerable moments.

On the other hand, John had thought of her safety before he'd thought of his own. He'd also tried to talk about himself—he was just woefully short on material from which to draw.

He didn't seem all that closed off.

Was the cost of his memory returning a change in his personality from the open, caring man she'd come to know back into a loner? Even now, there was an element of loss about him, and she'd just assumed it was because he was sailing around in his life without a rudder while being buffeted by dreadful suspicions about his character. But wait a second, wasn't character the one thing that amnesia wouldn't affect?

Using her teeth—the best tool in the world—she squeezed the last little link tighter. She dangled the owl in front of her face for a second, admiring its yellow eyes and the fine-tooled gold tips of its wings.

Okay, how about John's nightmares and the over-the-top thing he had about owls? That had to go back to his childhood, and she wanted to know how. It was a mystery, that and the burns…where and why and how. She had to know.

As she dropped the necklace over her head, the bathroom door opened. The owl dropped down under her T-shirt, out of view.

He was wearing what appeared to be flannel boxers and nothing else. She'd seen him bare-chested once before, when he'd run out into the snow to keep her from driving away that first morning. She noticed once again the power of his shoulders, the muscles and well-defined abs. Now she noticed he had great legs. She bet he could run like the wind.

He smiled at her and asked if she was ready for him to turn off the lights. She zipped the cuticle scissors and tweezers back into her makeup kit and set it aside as she pulled the covers up over her legs. "Go ahead," she said.

He lay down next to her in the dark. Paige kept to her own side, painfully aware of him, wishing she could sleep.

"Funny thing," he said after a few minutes, "how you can be dead tired and still wide awake."

"I know," she said.

The tired springs creaked as he changed position. "Now I'm sorry I promised not to compromise your virtue," he added.

She smiled, turning her head. She could barely make out his features. "So am I."

"Are you?"

There was a tone to his voice that caught her attention and she rolled onto her side, supporting her head with her bent arm. "You sound dubious."

He was quiet long enough for her to get a little tense. "Brian," he said at last.

"What does Brian—"

"I was there today, remember?" he said, his voice soft. "I saw the way you reacted when you saw him."

"He'd been hurt and it was because of me. You're not the only one who feels guilty for involving innocent people, you know."

"I don't mean that. I mean when he grabbed you and buried his head against you. The expression on your face was one of pure bliss."

She started to protest but sighed instead. "I had a moment of happiness, you're right, I admit it," she said.

"You thought he loved you," John whispered. His fingers grazed her face, so she knew he felt the tear that had rolled down her cheek. "I'm sorry," he added.

"Sorry?"

"That it didn't work out. I hate to see you crying over him."

"I'm not crying over him," she said.

"You're not?"

She put her hand over his fingers and pressed them against her lips. "Oh, John. Haven't you ever lost something or someone with such abruptness that it took your breath away? And no matter how angry you are at that person or how cheated you feel, there's a small part of you that aches for things to go back to the way they were."

"I don't know if I've ever felt that way," he said.

"I'll wager you have. I think everyone has. I don't know if it's the human reluctance to accept change, to fight for the status quo or what, but in that moment when I thought Brian still cared, it was like someone had given me back the last eighteen months of my life. Everything was right again, everything made sense."

"And when you realized he still cared about Jasmine?"

"It gutted me. But the important thing to remember is I would have come around all by myself when good sense triumphed over weakness. Do I love Brian? Do I want a man who left me for another woman, who is capable of deluding himself and me that way? No, thanks. I don't."

"Which begs the question," John said as his lips brushed her forehead, "what are you doing in bed with me?"

"I'm having a moment," she said, raising her head a little so his lips would connect with hers. "Stop talking so much."

The kiss was warm and sexy, romantic, actually, in a way none of their other kisses had been. Maybe it was the sense of time out of time—both the police and Korenev seemed a million miles away from this makeshift cocoon. It was as if they were in a tower, safe, alone, the whole world asleep far below them. There was just John with his shower-hot skin and lips that burned, with hands that touched her with authority, as though he'd known her forever.

She remembered the owl pendant as his hands caressed her bare stomach, and she sat up. In one determined gesture, she pulled the necklace over her head and dropped it to the carpeted floor, then pulled off her T-shirt.

His hands traveled up her waist until he cupped her breasts. "I was right," he said, his whispered breath hot against her skin. "Breathtaking."

She ran her hands across his shoulders. Any concern she might be hurting him as her hands glided over the satin-soft skin of the old burn scars was short-lived as he groaned in pleasure. His shorts and her sweatpants soon joined the other clothes on the floor, and for a second, they faced each other on their knees, more shadow than substance until he pulled her down on top of him. She had no illusions of forever—just of tonight. Tonight was enough.

And that was about the last quasicoherent thought she had for a while. The world went from drowsy kingdom to sensual overload as he caressed her backside and lowered his head to suck on her nipples, his mouth hot and demanding. As his fingers slid inside her, she found his erection and moments later gloried in the sensation they created as their bodies merged.

She hadn't had that many lovers in her life, and she'd never had one like him. His passion was insatiable, and it awakened things in her that she'd caught only glimpses of before, like vague sightings of a Yeti or a starlit image of the Loch Ness Monster. He shone light on the womanly parts of her that had been buried in the dark, and when she climaxed, it was a joyous combination of release and empowerment.

It wasn't until she was satisfied that John let go of his control and, rising to meet his needs, a true sense of power flooded her. He was lost in her body. He was hers for that moment. There were tears in her eyes as he shouted out in excitement and collapsed into her arms, his hot skin melding with her own.

They fell asleep entwined with each other, naked and satiated. In all that warm afterglow, Paige completely forgot to worry about morning.

That oversight caught up with her at daybreak, when she opened her eyes to find herself alone. The door was open and cold air blew into the room.

She dressed quickly, searching the rug for a

moment, sure she'd dropped the owl necklace on the floor the night before. It must have landed under the bed—she would look for it later. She pulled on shoes and peeked out the door.

No police. No Korenev. Just one car now, a red coupe parked three doors down, right where it had been the night before.

What if John had driven off in her car and left her here?

She ran around to the back of the motel and there was her car, right where they'd parked it in the wee dark hours of the morning.

The weather had changed—the wind was driving cold, icy drops against her skin, the clouds above were dark and ponderous. She turned a complete circle, searching for some sign of John, and found nothing but a Dumpster, a few trees and, through them, the glimmer of water.

She walked around to the front of the building and perused the road and the only other building she could see. It appeared to be a gas station but it wasn't open yet. Beyond that, the road disappeared into heavy forest.

Paige went back to their room, which was still profoundly empty. She looked for her necklace but it was gone, and all of a sudden, the fact it and John were both MIA seemed portentous. This time she grabbed her coat and the keys to the room, locking it behind her. She walked by the office just in case the bearded man was up and about, but through the window she could see it, too, was empty. She kept going around to the back. From this approach, she spied a trail leading through the trees toward the water, and for lack of a better plan she followed it.

The path ended on the shores of a small lake half-frozen-over with ice. Trees grew down to the water's edge, their limbs dark and bare like wizened fingers hanging low over the frozen water. There was a short pier. John stood on the end, dressed in jeans and a black T-shirt, no jacket, fists clenched at his sides. Tree limbs over his head appeared to reach down for him.

For one instant, the graphic artist inside her reared up its inner eye, and she instantly knew she would scrap what she'd been working on for the Red Hook album and use this image instead. She'd keep all these grays and blacks, merge red into the trees, put the three musicians on the pier. It was perfect. She took her cell phone from her pocket and snapped a quick photo.

Sliding the phone back into her pocket, she called John's name but he didn't turn. Unsure if he was in a trance, she approached warily. The dock was slippery, and the icy cover of the lake beneath it looked as though it would break if something heavy fell on it.

When she got close enough, Paige said John's name again and reached for his right hand. The glitter of a gold chain sparkled from between his fingers.

He turned to her; his eyes looked unfocused. This did nothing to negate the overwhelming male power of his presence, and for once dressed in his own clothes, clean and shaven, he appeared even stronger than he had before, leaner, more powerful, like a warrior. She felt a rush of desire that clouded her vision.

"What are you doing out here?" she asked. Chattering teeth were not entirely due to the cold.

He blinked but didn't respond, and for a second she was frightened. He was a lot bigger than she was, and there was that peculiar look in his eyes....

"John, come back to me," she whispered.

He lowered his head until his nose pressed against her cheek, then dipped lower, his breath hot on her neck.

"John?" she repeated, pulling away just far enough to see his face. "Are you in there, honey?"

He blinked again and shook his head as though to clear his mind. The fuzzy, unfocused look slipped away, replaced with his usual disarming gaze. The old John was back. "You shouldn't be out here. It's dangerous," he said.

"I agree. Let's—"

He withdrew his hand from hers and opened it between them, staring horrified at the owl that lay in his palm. He dropped it as though it was a hot coal. Paige managed to hook the chain before it fell to the dock and slipped between the cracks.

"Where did I get that?" he asked. As he spoke, he rubbed his palm against the denim of his jeans as though scratching an itch.

"You must have found it when you looked for your clothes," she said, pocketing the necklace and promising herself she'd lock it away in her suitcase as long as she stayed with John.

He looked down at himself as though checking out his clothes. It was obvious to Paige that he didn't remember getting dressed.

"Did you have another dream?" she asked.

He nodded.

"The same as before?"

"I think so. Except there was a part of the dream that was really nice. You and I made love."

She must have frowned, because he suddenly leaned over and cupped her chin. "I'm just teasing, Paige," he said, kissing her lips. "I know it wasn't a dream. Your scent is all over me, driving me crazy." The next thing she knew, he'd picked her up and was carrying her off the dock, his mouth locked on hers. If he slipped and they both fell onto the ice, they'd probably break through and drown.

She didn't really care. She was his for the taking, anytime, anywhere.

But he set her down once they were ashore and stared down into her eyes.

"How long have you been out here, John? Aren't you freezing?" she asked.

"Now that you mention it, yeah, I am," he said, but he cradled her face in his hands and kissed her again.

"Why did you come to the lake? How did you even know there was a lake?"

"I didn't know. I don't know how I got here."

"But the dream…"

He cast her a look and sighed, running a hand through his hair.

"You don't want to talk about all this, do you?" she said.

His hand slid down her arm until he grasped her hand, and they began walking down the path toward the motel. "About what? Me waking up in a cold sweat, grabbing for clothes in the dark, running like crazy while owls swooped down over my head, stopping in the nick of time before I catapulted myself off a pier? No, come to think of it, I don't want to talk about it. There's nothing to say except I'm running like hell, every night it seems, trying to get away, and I have a horrible feeling what I'm trying to get away from is myself."

She did her best not to look alarmed, but cripes. Natalie had said he had closed doors. Just what was behind those doors, and would either of them survive his finding out?

"I can't believe I slept through you leaving," she said to fill the emptiness. The only sound was of their feet crunching against icy ground, and she suspected the sound grated on his nerves as much as it did on hers. "When I woke up and saw that open door, it scared the hell out of me."

He stopped and turned her to face him. "I left the door open?"

"Uh-huh."

He shook his head. "I can't believe I was so self-involved I left you asleep and alone in a room with an open door. With a mad killer on the loose, no less. I'm beginning to think I really do belong in a loony bin."

She wasn't sure she didn't agree. "We should get out of here," she said. "Carol Ann Oates is only a few hours away."

"You're going to think I'm a chicken, but I'm almost afraid what she might have to say about me."

Once again, Paige kept her thoughts to herself. Last night she'd been so sure about him, but after this morning, she had to ask herself a couple of cold, hard questions.

Was she allowing her emotional needs to trump her common sense?

Was she using John to forget her own past?

In essence, was she just like him, two peas in the old pod, both of them running, both reluctant to stop and catch a breath, both afraid of what would happen if ever they did?

Chapter Eleven

They reached Seeley Lake in the early afternoon. Deer Creek Spa turned out to be several miles from the actual town, located on acres of forested land that was reached after crossing a quaint bridge. The spa consisted of a main lodge and several nearby buildings, including smaller ones that appeared to be individual cabins. Each was constructed of ponderosa-pine logs with steep green metal roofs. Walkways connected all the buildings to each other, ending in ramps leading to each covered porch.

"This doesn't look like a place for sick people, does it?" Paige asked.

"No. Is there a chance you misunderstood Mademoiselle Batiste? Could Carol Ann just be vacationing?"

"I don't think so, but she did have a really thick accent and my French is rusty at best."

"When this is all over, let's go to France. You can brush up on your language skills."

He said it with a smile, as if it was a joke, but she put a hand on his arm. "And what will you do?"

"I'll visit the market and buy wonderful food and cook it for you, then I'll take you to bed and make love to you for hours."

She fanned her face. "Okay, you're on. France it is."

There was still a smattering of snow on the grassy ground around the buildings. They followed the road past an exit earmarked for visitor parking, pulling in behind a delivery truck toward the back of the building. Signs pointed the way to the office, which was located inside the doors of the lodge.

The lobby was enormous, with several offices opening off of it and elevators leading up to a second-story mezzanine. Several people, some in wheelchairs, sat around a circular, freestanding fireplace while a man with a soft-looking red beard read from a thin book using a mellow, soft voice. Many of the listeners seemed to be asleep, but some nodded as though his words held great meaning for them.

"May I help you?"

The inquiry came from a short, freckled young woman with a strawberry blond ponytail and a serious-looking pair of black-framed glasses perched on her button nose. Holding a clipboard, she looked like a child playing receptionist.

"We're looking for Carol Ann Oates," John said.

"And you are?"

"Friends."

"I'm sorry, but we have strict rules here. Absolutely no unannounced or unexpected visitors. I can't even worry Ms. Oates with your presence. She's left strict orders to be left alone except by the people on her list."

"Who's on her list?" Paige asked.

"I don't know. No one has ever come to see her so I've never looked. Everyone has to make out a list, though."

"Could you look?" John said. "Maybe we could speak to one of her contacts."

"Let me just call up her file on the computer." She moved around the big wood counter and tapped on the computer keys. "Ms. Oates just has one contact and he's not a local," she said. "John Cinca." She wrinkled her nose and added, "I don't know why but that name seems familiar. Anyway, there's a phone number here. It looks like we tried to call him two days ago but he didn't answer his phone. I'll copy the number for you—"

"Don't bother," John interrupted. "I'm John Cinca. I lost my phone." It was obvious to Paige he expected the diminutive receptionist to point a finger and accuse him of murder right there on the spot.

But how did John get to be the only name on the older woman's contact list? Natalie had said he'd gone to see a relative in Canada. But they apparently hadn't been close during his life, so why now all of a sudden?

Paige and John exchanged worried glances. No way to talk things out in front of the receptionist. It would have to wait.

"Do you have proof of your identity?" the receptionist asked.

"I lost my driver's license in the same accident that got my phone. I do have this, however," John said as he withdrew his passport he'd taken from the manila envelope and handed it to her. She studied the picture, then John's face.

"Okay," she said, handing him back his passport. "But you'll have to speak to her doctor first. I'll see if Dr. Ming is in his office."

After a quick phone call, the receptionist turned back to them. "He said I should send you right over," she said. "He's actually with Ms. Oates right now." She whipped out a piece of pink paper and, using a pen, circled the lodge and a small building across the grounds, tracing the path between them with ink. "She's in Hawk's Hollow. Use the back door over there.

It makes finding it easier. You can wait for him here, miss."

Paige had started walking away with John and paused upon hearing the last comment. "I can't go with him?" she asked, turning.

"I'm sorry. You're not on the list. You can wait here, though."

"No, thanks, I'll wait in the car," Paige said, turning back to John.

"Are you sure?" he asked. "It's pretty cold."

She answered in a soft voice. "This place kind of gives me the willies. I'll be okay."

"I shouldn't be long."

"Take your time. I'll work on my project."

HE LEFT THROUGH THE BACK door and picked up his pace. Across the way, he saw Paige unlocking the door of her car and scooting inside. It felt weird to be without her.

No time for dawdling. Sooner or later, that receptionist would figure out where she'd heard his name before—like on the news. He wanted to be long gone before then.

The doctor met him on the front porch of Hawk's Hollow. He was an Asian man of fifty or so, his black hair streaked with gunmetal gray. He, too, wore black-framed glasses. Perhaps that was the compulsory style for any Deer Creek staff member who needed vision correction.

He was dressed casually just like everyone else here. No uniforms, no lab coats, no dangling stethoscopes.

John kept the introduction short and sweet. He was aching to ask the doctor if the man knew why John's name was on Carol Ann Oates's list of contacts but was almost certain that would arouse suspicion. So far the man didn't seem to make any connections to the name John Cinca, and that was good.

"I wasn't aware your aunt had made allowances for visitors. I'm sure glad she did," the doctor said.

His aunt. At last, someone he could talk to. "How is she?" John asked.

"Terminal. And that's not something we say lightly around here. Our credo is as long as there's life, there's hope. There are many worthwhile alternatives to mainstream medicine. But Carol Ann is very ill, and even she knew when she came to us this time it was to have a place to die on her own terms."

"Then she's been here before?"

"Twice. Her disease was diagnosed late last summer and she came immediately. I had great expectations our treatments would work. She went home, but returned after the holidays. Things had gotten worse, but once again, we were hopeful. Then she called a week ago and asked if she could come here one more time. I knew why, and as I said, so did she. I gather she's alone up in Canada. Never married, as you know. Carol Ann is wealthy, capable and fiercely independent, not the kind to suffer fools kindly."

"But she didn't want to die alone," John said.

Dr. Ming nodded. "While I hope your presence can give your aunt some sense of peace, I have to warn you that she's in and out of consciousness and on some pretty high-level painkillers, so she's not always coherent. Lila, her nurse, is in there with her. Someone is always with her. Limit your visit to ten minutes, please."

He walked down the ramp toward the lodge, his shoulders stooped as though the burden of failing to find a miracle for a patient weighed heavy on him. John took a deep breath and let himself into the darkened room.

A large woman sat in a chair in the corner, knitting needles flashing as she worked on something big enough to cover her lap. She looked up as John entered.

The room was warm and a bit stuffy, the furnishings sparse but expensive. The aroma of fresh flowers in a vase competed with the odor of medications and illness.

The most defining element of the room was the state-of-the-art adjustable bed. The woman tucked under the covers was about the same color as the bleached sheets.

John approached warily, not sure what he would find, half hoping and half dreading that one look at this woman would bring recollection crashing into his head or that she would rise and point a finger and tell him why children screamed accusations in his dreams.

Carol Ann Oates wasn't as old as John had expected. Sixty, maybe a little older. Her hair was dark brown with long gray roots, her features sharp in her thin face. She looked as though she might be an uncompromising woman when she wasn't hovering near death. For now, she lay very still, the rattling sound of her breathing the only sign she lived.

While her pallor and thinness were alarming, she didn't seem to be in any pain. John peered at her face in an attempt to see a family resemblance with himself or even with the photograph of the grandparents who had raised him, but he wasn't even sure those were her parents. He found nothing familiar in her features.

Could his aunt explain where all the money in the bank came from and what had happened to him as a child? "I'll be back here in ten minutes," the woman in the corner whispered as she rose and set aside her knitting. "I could use a breath of fresh air."

John nodded. He was glad not to have to ask questions—if Carol Ann ever woke up—in front of a stranger. Unsure exactly how to proceed, he once again wished Paige were with him. He had a feeling she would instinctively know just how to go about this.

For a second, as he stared out the window, he was back at the little lake behind the motel, standing out on the dock, looking down at Paige, not sure who she was, just knowing she was important to him. He'd nuzzled her neck, inhaling her scent, wanting her desperately.

He closed his eyes as images of their lovemaking washed through him like cleansing rain.

His eyes startled open when a hand clenched his wrist. He jerked, looking down. Carol Ann was awake and staring up at him.

Her eyes were as dark as her dyed hair, piercing in her sallow face. "Charles?" she whispered in a reed-thin voice.

With his free hand, John pulled a chair up close to his aunt's side and sat down. "Not Charles," he said gently. "John."

She concentrated on his face. "Look so alike… You're the hero…" she mumbled.

She'd contacted him after the incident with the congressman; that must be what the hero thing was about. "Who is Charles?" he asked.

Her fingers shook against his wrist and her

thin lips trembled. It was obvious to John she was agitated, and he patted her bony arm to try to comfort her. "It's okay, you don't have to think about him if you don't want to. Can you tell me what you contacted me about? I've forgotten but I know it was important."

Her eyes suddenly focused on his and this time when she spoke, she seemed more lucid. "Did you…did you find them? Cole and Tyler? Did you?"

"Cole and Tyler?" More names?

Tears gathered in her eyes, trickled down her gaunt cheeks.

"So many wasted years," she said. "My fault."

"Why is it your fault?"

She shook her head. "So lost…"

This was going nowhere. He had to try to get her to focus. Who were all these people? Was this the drugs talking, or were these other family members?

"Aunt Carol, you contacted me before, remember? After you read about me in the paper, you called. Why did you call?"

Her brow wrinkled in concentration. Finally, she said, "Charles? Is that you?"

Back to names. No more names, he wanted to tell her. "No, it's me, John. John Cinca, remember?"

She narrowed her eyes as she stared up at

him, and then her grip on his wrist finally slacked and her eyes closed. "Daddy disowned you," she whispered. "Go away."

He glanced at his watch. The nurse would be back in a few moments. As he struggled to figure out what to do next, a rattling noise like something scratching against the glass came from the window. Settling his aunt's frail hand on the blanket, he crossed the room. Paige stood outside. She held aloft a small branch that she'd found to touch the glass, as the window was a good four feet above her head.

The window was the kind that lifted from the bottom. He inched it up.

"What's wrong?" he asked, heartbeat tripling as he took in the spooked expression on her face.

"He's here," she whispered frantically.

"Who?"

"Korenev. I saw him drive up."

"Did he see you?"

"We were parked behind that truck. I don't think he saw the car. He couldn't have or he would have come after me."

"Are you sure it's him?"

"In that van, are you kidding? Anyway, he parked a few spots away and limped into the lodge. He was wearing a different disguise this time, but it was him, all right. I moved the car close by. Hurry, you have to come right now."

He started to lower the window. "I'll be right out."

"If you go out the front way, someone will see you. Come through the window. Just hurry."

John turned back into the room, taking one lingering look at his aunt. She hadn't wanted to die alone, something he understood on a gut level in a way he probably hadn't before losing his memory. He doubted he'd ever see her again, and that loss joined all the others gnawing at him. She'd been his one good chance of understanding, and he wished he could stay here with her, keeping a silent and unseen vigil until the end.

"John?" Paige whispered. "I hear voices coming from the sidewalk. Hurry. Please."

"Goodbye, Aunt Carol Ann," he said, but she was asleep and didn't react. Turning, he drew the sash the rest of the way up and climbed through the window, dropping to the ground in a heap and scrambling to his feet. Paige caught his hand and they ran across the grounds.

She had parked behind another cottage and they all but dived into the car, but they drove off in a sedate manner, as though they weren't trying to outrun a killer, trying to appear innocent and leisurely when their pulses alone could power a rocket to the moon.

"I HALF EXPECTED THE WOMAN at the counter to alert the police, but how did Korenev find us?" John demanded.

Paige had been wondering the same thing.

"Turn left, we need to get off the main road. Hell, we need to disappear."

"How do we do that?" Paige asked, turning left onto a smaller road.

"I don't know."

"Maybe when he ransacked your place he found something that led him to Carol Ann."

"Maybe, but how did he know she was in Montana?"

"Okay, maybe he called Mademoiselle Batiste, who mentioned having spoken to us."

John shook his head. "Maybe, but it seems really remote. The woman told you she wouldn't talk to a man about my aunt's whereabouts."

Paige slid him a glance. "Your aunt?"

"Yeah. I have an aunt, or will for a while. She's terminal."

"I'm sorry. Did you learn anything from her?"

"No. She thought I was someone named Charles or Cole or Tyler—she was a little out of it. Damn, Paige, how did Korenev know where we were?"

"He's been one step ahead or one step behind all the way," she said.

"But those steps were based on logical conclusions to be drawn from what you told him, what he heard on the radio or what he knew about me. This is different."

"It's like he followed us here," she said, "but if that was the case, he could have attacked us at the motel."

"Maybe it took him a while to get that leg fixed up. Wait a second. Pull the car over."

They had just rounded a turn and were now skirting Seeley Lake, which spread to their left. The right side of the road was heavily forested. "Where?"

"Anywhere."

"But there's no cover here. If he comes around that corner, he'll see us."

"I don't think it matters. I think he sees us all the time. Pull over. Hurry."

Paige pulled onto the verge. John was out of the car before it fully stopped. She stayed behind the wheel with the engine running, her gaze glued to the rearview mirror. John walked around the car, pausing every few inches to lean down and feel around. She finally rolled down her window to ask what he was doing.

"John?"

As he approached her window, he opened his

hand to reveal two small black boxes affixed to a magnetic strip.

"What are those?"

"Tracking devices. Korenev must have planted them on your car outside my warehouse while we were preoccupied looking at photographs or something. Before he broke down the front gate, you know, just in case we weren't inside or got away. One was fixed to the undercarriage behind the back bumper, the other one up under the same wheel well where you put your spare key as a matter of fact."

"But two?"

"He probably figured we'd stop looking once we uncovered one of them. That's how he found us. He couldn't walk into the hospital with a gunshot wound because they'd report it, so he'd have to take the time to find someone to help him who wouldn't talk. He just took his time getting his leg fixed and then followed the yellow brick road right to our doorstep."

"Could there be more?"

"Not where he could have easily stuck them. I'd say probably not." He threw both devices over the top of the car into the forest. "Let's get as far away from here as we can," he said as he scooted back inside. "Drive fast."

"Where do we go now?" Paige asked.

"Missoula has the closest international airport?"

"I think so. Why?"

"You said there were important papers in those boxes you brought from your apartment," he said. "Does that include your passport?"

"Yes, why? Oh, wait, I get it. We're going to Kanistan. Will you be able to get on an airplane? Won't they have your name or something? If you do get out of the country, will you be able to get back in?"

"The answers to your questions are I don't know, I don't know and I don't know. But I also don't know where else to go from here. If I get caught, I get caught."

"You're turning into a fatalist."

He'd been looking out the back window—no need to ask who or what he was looking for—but turned back to her now.

"Stop at the first store that might sell a prepaid cell phone, will you? I need to borrow more money. Do you have credit cards? I'll pay you back."

"I know you will. I saw your bank account."

"Speaking of the bank account, Paige, has it occurred to you that Korenev could be a hit man of some kind and that he could be coming after money I stole from someone or took as a bribe and then didn't deliver what I'd promised? Or the money could be his? We could have been partners or something. The timing all seems to fit."

"I hadn't thought of that."

He shook his head. "I have."

"I can see that. But that's because we disagree about *you*."

"What do you mean?"

She glanced at him again. "I think you're a decent guy with indecent problems. You think you're a thief and a scoundrel and a crook—or worse."

"Hmm…"

"And if you're right about any of that, then why hasn't Korenev even asked you for the money or demanded it back? He just seems hellbent on destroying you."

"I don't know," John said. "Which seems to be my catchphrase."

They'd just entered the small town of Seeley and it appeared the pickings for something like a phone might be limited until they spied a new drugstore. They went inside and found exactly one pay-as-you-go model. Paige waited until they were back in the car before she asked John why he couldn't just use hers.

"I want one that won't trace back to either of us."

"Because?"

"The police are about to get an anonymous tip about the current whereabouts of Anatola Korenev."

Chapter Twelve

In Missoula, they stopped at a coffee shop for a late lunch. While John figured out how to get a tip to the people where it would do some good, his gaze never strayed far from Paige, who had found a power outlet and was busily booting up her laptop.

Had he ever cared about a woman the way he was beginning to care for her? Had anyone ever been as good a friend or lover, been as generous as she was? And what had he given her in return?

Well, he'd almost gotten her stabbed, shot, mutilated, her sister hurt, her old boyfriend mugged, and look at the way she kept glancing at the door as though waiting for a killer to walk through it with a pronounced limp and a missing finger.

All thanks to him.

He had to figure this out, get his memory back and reassure himself he was exactly the man he hoped he was minus all the confusion and doubts. He wanted reasonable explanations for his bizarre dreams and seemingly shady behavior. He wanted to find out if he and Paige could build something together that wasn't fueled by mutual terror.

When he completed his call, he returned to the table. She tore her gaze from the door and looked up at him, producing a smile. "Good news. Kanistan does not require a visa. We have two tickets to New York and connecting flights to Kanistan. Only one plane a day goes there and it leaves New York at midnight, so connecting flight times are going to be tight. Bad news. We either return the very next day or we stay a week. I booked the next day."

"That probably explains my short visit last time," John said, not voicing his first thought, and that was if he was still wanted for murder, it was likely they'd never even make it to New York, let alone Kanistan. His stomach knotted at the thought of being taken into custody, or maybe it knotted because he was allowing Paige to travel with him and who knew what they would find—or who would find them. Instead, he said, "One day should be enough. This is the end of the road for me. I feel it coming to a head. I either find out the truth or I go to the cops."

"I looked up news in Lone Tree, as well," she

continued. "The paper said the body of a retired fire chief was found in the residence of John Cinca. They also mentioned the gunfire and all that. Speculation is that you're dead."

"They'll find Korenev's fingerprints somewhere in that place," John said. "I'm beginning to believe I may not rot in jail, after all."

They ate sandwiches in a hurry, then made their way to the airport, where they parked Paige's car in long-term parking in case they had trouble getting back to it. They stuck all their gear except for an overnight bag in the trunk, including John's weapon.

Once inside the terminal, Paige called her sister, who didn't answer her phone, and then tried Matt. He also didn't answer. John spent the time on the lookout for security officers or anyone else who paid him undo attention.

As Paige pocketed her phone, he noticed she looked upset. Once again, he sought to set her free of this crazy ride-along role she'd taken with such conviction. "It's okay if you go home," he said.

She looked at him as though startled from thought. "What?"

"Home. If you need to go home, go. I'll take care of Kanistan and you take care of your family. I'll call you when I get there and tell you what I find—"

"Hold that thought," Paige said. "Why didn't I think to call home? As in my mother, I mean. She should be home."

Paige pulled out her cell again and made the call, relief evident in her voice as she launched into a conversation with someone, probably her mother.

When she hung up a couple of minutes later, she gave a brief report. "Mom hasn't seen Katy in a few days but didn't expect to because of the move. She says no news is good news and she'll go check on her at her new place tomorrow and call me back. Oh, and she's devastated for me about what happened at the wedding and wants me to come home so the two of us can go over to Brian's place and tell Jasmine what we think of her. And lastly, her current boyfriend asked her to marry him yesterday and she said yes and wants me to be maid of honor—again."

"She sounds like a character," John said.

"That's one way to put it. Okay, now tell me what we're going to do in Kanistan."

"We're going to that town near the island with the hotel. We're going to find Sergi and Galina Ogneva."

"Your grandparents."

"Yes. I went to Kanistan a few weeks ago. It must have been to see and talk to them. They can tell me about my past and why I visited recently. It's all I can think to do."

"If they're still alive."

"We'll take it as it comes. And they must have been alive if I went to see them a few weeks ago."

"You're assuming it's them you went to see."

"True." He shrugged. "What other option do I have?"

"None."

THERE WAS A TENSE MOMENT when officials perused John's passport, but no guns were drawn, no handcuffs produced. They both fell into exhausted silence within an hour of taking off out of New York, knowing when they landed they would have lost hours.

It took John longer to fall asleep than it did Paige, and for a while he sat with his head back, studying her as she slept against his shoulder. Even from the angle of slightly above and looking down at her, she was perfect. The sweep of her lashes against her porcelain cheek, the shape of her nose and curve of her lips made him burn with the desire to tilt her face up to his and brush his lips against hers, to feel her closer, in his arms, make her his again, over and over.

How well did he really know her? Was she really over Brian, or was she fooling herself?

If she was using him to disconnect with that guy, did it matter? Wasn't he using her to try to stay sane?

Or was there something more growing between them, and whatever it was could it survive the transformations that would inevitably come when he recovered? One fervent wish: please, let there be no other woman in his life, waiting somewhere to know his fate. It seemed unlikely given what Natalie said about him, but sometimes old girlfriends were the last to know about new ones.

He scrunched down and kissed Paige's forehead, and she half smiled and made a soft sound that drove his libido straight through the cabin roof. He had to settle for closing his hand over hers. Eventually, he closed his eyes and drifted back to sleep.

And he was walking. It was dark. Then he was in a room and there was a knock on the door and he answered it. A clown stood there, a clown with a big red nose and a blue ruffled collar. A clown with bright yellow shoes, huge shoes! He held a present in his hands, one with bows and ribbons. He gave it to John.

The door slammed. And then the owls came, wings beating. He threw up his arms and the present rose into the air above his head and ex-

ploded into a million little stars. He had to run.
The owls were coming—

"John!"

The voice was soft but urgent, and he opened
his eyes at once. The wings still beat, but Paige
was there and she had her arms around him as
much as she could given their seating.

He stared into her eyes, and then his gaze
shifted to the red line from the chain that had
choked her when she pulled it from around
her neck. The owl was right there, under her
clothes, nestled between her luscious breasts.
He touched the old wound gingerly, then slid his
fingers down her throat, moving aside the fabric
until the gold chain sparkled against her skin....

She caught his hand and held it very tight in
hers. She said something, but her voice was just
a soft purr, soothing but indistinct.

She pressed her lips to his cheek and he
shifted his head so their lips came into contact.
He kissed her with all the fire that raged in his
body, his hands grasping her closer, desperate
to get past her clothes and touch her cool skin
and tear away that owl.

With a gentle but firm shove, she pushed him
away.

He took a deep breath and swallowed, straight-
ening in his seat as she readjusted her clothes.

He'd been willing to strip her bare on a plane

full of people. "You better lock me up," he muttered.

"I have bigger and better plans for you," she said with an uneasy smile. "But not until we get a hotel room." It seemed to him she was trying to make light of something that had alarmed her, and he closed his eyes.

After several seconds of silence, she squeezed his hand and, leaning close, whispered into his ear. "It's okay, John. I'm right here. I'm not going anywhere."

Opening his eyes, he tried a smile. It seemed to crack his face as though he'd never smiled before, and he took another deep breath and nodded.

The steward came around with hot coffee soon after that and then a light breakfast. The images of the dream faded as they always did, but he knew they'd be back.

UPON LANDING IN THE LARGE city of Traterg, they hired a car and driver at the airport to take them to an outlying village over a hundred miles away called Slovo.

It was cold and gray outside, rain turning into sleet as they traveled higher in elevation. John leaned over the seat and talked to the driver in fractured English. The man was young with glossy, curly black hair and bright red suspenders.

As they spoke, Paige sat back. She felt numb from the inside out. And when she tried to figure out exactly how she'd come to be at this place in this time with this man, it left her breathless.

Growing up, her mother had been so flighty and her sister so like her mother that it had fallen to Paige to be the sensible one, and after her father finally got tired of all the drama and left the family, Paige took on his roles, as well. When she was old enough, she drove her sister to and from activities, and did most of the cooking and cleaning because her mother was usually in the middle of a disastrous and time-consuming relationship and otherwise occupied.

Then Paige had left home, gone to school and graduated and proceeded to carve a little place for herself, building up a client base and gaining a good word-of-mouth reputation. The one silly thing she'd done was move into an apartment with her sister upon Katy's urging, and that had served as a vivid reminder of how chaotic living with one of her family members could be. When Brian and she decided to get married, it had seemed life would now unfold in front of her in a stable, predictable pattern.

Paige sighed as she looked out the window. Common sense said she was being an idiot when it came to John. In her saner moments, she wondered if she found something familiar and kind of oddly safe in the danger that nipped at their heels. Wasn't this kind of reminiscent of the way she grew up, only with way-higher stakes?

"Dmitry here says the lake we're going to was carved out of the land when a glacier retreated umpteen years ago and melted ice filled the basin it left behind," John said. "The hotel is on the island. Slovo is on this side of the lake. He says it's more like a village than a city."

"There's the bridge," Paige said, leaning forward and gesturing at the green turrets visible through the rain-spattered windows.

And all of a sudden this seemed like the most naive trip in the world to her. This was a holiday destination. What in the world made them think that his grandparents lived here now or ever had? The photo had probably been taken during a vacation.

They arrived in Slovo in the late afternoon when the waning light made the wet cobblestone streets appear like black ice. Across the lake, as viewed through the driving sleet, the island hotel resembled a medieval fortress instead of the ice-crystal castle in the photo Paige had used years before.

"The village seems small enough that someone might know of them," John said. "I mean

I have to assume that when I was here a few weeks ago I knew where to find them. This time I'll have to search."

She heard the excitement in his voice and crossed mental fingers that he would find these long-lost grandparents who would fill him in on his missing childhood and explain the visit he'd made earlier that year.

And then that the nightmares would stop. Those were getting a little spooky.

"Let's start at the post office," John told Dmitry as they wound their way through the narrow streets.

"Posta?"

"Yes. Please, that would be great."

"Does any of this look even vaguely familiar?" Paige asked as they parked in front of a modest stone building.

"Not even a little, but what's new?"

Dmitry went into the post office with them. Two women and one man were busy sorting mail behind a well-worn counter. The small lobby area was empty of customers but looked similar to the old small-town post offices she'd seen in movies.

Leaning against the counter, Dmitry spoke rapidly and with enthusiasm to the man who had come to help. The two women left their tasks and wandered over to listen. "I tell them you are grandson," Dmitry said in an aside to John. "Looking for the grandma and grandpa. Man say you look familiar."

John smiled. "Really? Has he seen me before, is that what he means?"

"Yes, yes. Before. Not sure where."

Everyone nodded and smiled, expressions warm and friendly as they waited expectantly, Paige assumed, for names.

"My grandparents' last name is Ogneva," John said. "Sergi and Galina Ogneva."

One woman's hand flew to cover her mouth. Her eyes above her knuckles watered. The other one gripped the edge of the counter and swayed on her feet while the man seemed to inhale his smile.

John looked from one of them to the other. "Wait a second, I have a picture of them," he said, and produced the snapshot taken over two decades before. "That's me in the middle," he told them. "I think I lived here years and years ago. With them. With my grandparents."

Everyone studied the photo but no one said anything.

Dmitry looked at John, shaking his head. "Something is wrong," he said.

No kidding. "Can you tell what's upset them?" Paige asked.

Dmitry spoke to them again. This time the

man kept glancing at John, but the women wouldn't meet his gaze. When Dmitry looked back at John, his eyes were sympathetic. "My friend, John, I have terrible news," the younger man began. "Grandpa and Grandma die in horrible fire."

The man behind the counter had more to say and Dmitry listened, translating once he'd finished. "Bullets, too."

"Bullets. What do you mean?"

"Bullets in bodies. This man say Sergi shoot his wife, set fire to his house and shoot himself. I am sorry."

John stood there, eyes wide, disbelief shadowing his face. "When did this happen?" he said at last.

Dmitry talked to the postal worker and reported back. "This man knows where he see you now. You were outside house with Galina five weeks ago. He hear you leave for Traterg and the night there be the fire."

"I can't believe we came all this way and they're dead," John said, looking at Paige, disappointment darkening his eyes.

She gripped his arm. "I know. I'm sorry."

John addressed Dmitry again. "Find out where the police station is."

While the conversation continued, Paige walked outside to the sidewalk. Standing close to the building, so the overhang would protect her from the weather, she watched the cars and people hurrying about the end of their day, on their way home, perhaps, or maybe on their way to meet with friends. Ordinary activities, things that made up the bulk of a life. Turning, she glanced inside the post-office window, and for a second John and the others appeared like silent actors on a stage.

What was she doing here?

John turned just then and their gazes locked and she smiled. Poor guy looked miserable and yet he was still concerned about where she'd gone off to and if she was okay. When this situation resolved itself, would she have to get to know a whole new John Cinca? And considering the fact that he'd apparently never recovered from his first bout of amnesia, was it possible he would not recover from this one, either?

Could she live with all the questions?

A minute later, John and Dmitry joined her on the sidewalk.

"Let's go," John said, putting his arm around Paige's shoulders. Dmitry opened the door and they piled inside.

"Where are we going?" Paige asked.

"The police station isn't far from here we're told."

Sure enough, Dmitry dropped them at another stone building a few blocks away, begging off going inside because the man in the post office had told them that there were English-speaking officers here. Paige got the impression Dmitry wasn't anxious to be around the cops.

The door emptied into a small lobby decorated with two benches, a garbage can and a standing ashtray. Through a glass door, they could see a counter and some more chairs. Several people sat in the chairs.

John held the door open for Paige and they entered to find a woman seated at a desk behind the counter, smoking a cigarette as she pecked away at a computer keyboard with two fingers. She looked up when they approached and rattled off something neither John or Paige could comprehend. The cigarette bobbed up and down as she spoke.

"English?" John asked hopefully.

She got up from the desk, walked to a closed door, knocked once and opened it without waiting. "Irina," she called. Then she went back to her desk.

A woman in her forties wearing a dark blue uniform emerged from the other room a few moments later. She had very black hair pulled straight back from her face and fastened into a bun at the nape of her neck. Icy blue eyes regarded John and Paige with speculation.

"How can I help you?" she asked in very good English.

John introduced himself and Paige before adding, "I was wondering what you could tell me about Galina and Sergi Ogneva."

"They are dead," the woman said.

"I realize that. The man at the post office told me."

"Why do you want to know about them?"

"I lived with them for several years when I was a boy," John said.

Irina narrowed her blue eyes and looked at him more closely. "You're Ivan?"

John looked at Paige. "Ivan?"

"That may be what John translates to here, like in Russian," she said.

Irina nodded. "That is so."

"Yes, then I guess I am," John said. "You knew me back then?"

"Yes," Irina said, her lips curving into a smile. "Although you've changed a lot, of course. I lived two houses away from your grandparents. You don't remember me, do you?"

"No, I'm afraid I don't."

Irina's eyes grew pensive. "You weren't a very happy boy," she said. "I was just a teenager, but even I could see that. Your grandparents weren't the real warm types. In fact, until you came, none of us even knew they had a child, let alone a grandchild. And then, of course, you didn't speak the language and they refused to teach you. My parents used to say…"

Her voice trailed off and she shrugged.

"How did I manage school if I couldn't speak the language?" John asked.

"They sent you to an English-speaking boarding school. You were really only in Slovo for a few weeks in the summer and that was just for three or four years."

"More like six," John said.

"I had gone off to college by then," Irina said with another shrug. She narrowed her eyes as she added, "I heard that you visited the Ognevas a month or so ago."

John nodded. "I was told the fire happened soon after I left."

"That night, as a matter of fact."

"I heard that. Do you know if I visited anyone else on that trip?"

"I do not," she said, her expression perplexed. "Wouldn't you remember if you had?"

"Ordinarily, but things are a little fuzzy right now. Listen, Irina, I was also told that Sergi shot Galina, set fire to his house and killed himself."

Irina arched her eyebrows, and when she spoke it sounded as though she chose her words with care. "Yes, that was the official finding."

There was a *but* in her voice no one could have missed.

"Do you have reason to believe otherwise?" John asked.

Irina looked over her shoulder toward the room she'd exited a few minutes before, then scanned the faces of the others in the waiting area.

"Meet me in the lobby," she said softly, then disappeared through yet another door. They left the office, aware of the expressions of those waiting.

Irina came into the lobby through a narrow door in the back and joined them on one of the benches. She kept her voice soft as she spoke. "You have to remember I knew Sergi my whole life. He was an arrogant man when he was young and Galina was very cold. But they had grown old and frail, well over eighty, you know. I cannot imagine either of them committing suicide or murder unless it was guilt brought about when you came home so suddenly. But then why destroy their house? It makes no sense."

"Is there any proof it happened another way?"

"Just a phone call," Irina said. "It was made earlier that night to an untraceable number in Traterg. My superior wrote it off. I tried to uncover who it was made to, but I gave up."

"You've no idea?"

"None."

"And your superior isn't concerned?"

Irina's shoulders lifted and dropped. In barely a whisper, she added, "He is new, a transplant from Traterg. I am not so sure he is completely honest."

"What do you think happened, Irina?" Paige said.

Irina studied their eyes for a second, then glanced over her shoulder as though to make sure they were alone. It seemed she was reluctant to say what she thought in any plainer terms.

"You're talking murder," John murmured.

Eyes wide, Irina nodded.

"But there's something else," Paige said.

John looked puzzled as he threw Paige a glance. "What do you mean, something else?"

"About your grandparents," Paige told him, then looked straight into Irina's eyes. "You started a thought a few minutes ago, and then you let it go. You said your parents used to say something. What did they used to say?"

Irina shook her head. "It was just gossip."

"I'd like to know," John said.

"But it probably isn't true."

"Still, I'd like to know."

"It was my mother," Irina said, looking down at her hands, then back at John. "I overheard her tell my father that Galina Ogneva once told another woman in the village that she found out when she was just a young woman that she couldn't have children but that she was fine with that. She said she didn't like children. And then a year later, you show up and are introduced as a long-lost orphaned grandson who couldn't remember a moment of his past."

"How did she explain me?" John asked.

"She told everyone she'd had a daughter who she gave to her sister to raise. Then that daughter married an American professor and the two of them died in a traffic accident and you were sent to live in Kanistan with her and Sergi."

"Did your mother believe her story?" Paige inquired.

Irina shrugged again. "I don't think so. But after all, it was a time of some trouble here—"

"What kind of trouble?" John interrupted.

"Well, let's see. It was a long time ago. Okay, there was a scandal concerning the police chief in Traterg that ruined his career. He was a war hero and everyone thought much of him. He committed suicide rather than face criminal investigation. Then two young mothers were shot by soldiers during a riot. Oh, and an ambassador and his whole family were killed and everyone thought it was the Russians."

"Was it?"

"No, turned out to be domestic. He was having an affair, the girl got pregnant, he got rid of her, her family retaliated…sordid stuff."

"Anything else?"

"Endless border disputes," she said with a sigh. "Every week the newspaper was filled with statistics about how many died on each side. It was a restless year, that's all I'm saying. People were distracted."

"So, in other words, no one knows who I really am."

Irina looked shocked for a second and then nodded. "Like I said, though, it started with a rumor, nothing more."

John thanked Irina and got to his feet, walking away with stiff legs.

The knot in Paige's stomach hinted the rumor was true. And just where did that leave John now?

Chapter Thirteen

That night they fell asleep on pink satin sheets
in a heart-shaped bed located in the honeymoon
suite at the Hotel Traterg. It had been the only
available room and they'd taken it without dis-
cussion, too tired and preoccupied to care about
the exorbitant price or the questionable decor.

They'd ordered dinner from room service,
eaten in numb silence, then fallen asleep after
sharing a few kisses, wrapped in each other's
arms, more for comfort than sex.

John awoke in the middle of the night. He'd
been dreaming but it wasn't about owls for a
change, and the trancelike disassociation he was
getting used to waking up with wasn't present.

He'd been dreaming about the people in
the photograph taken beside the bridge. It had
been hot outside and he'd been swimming in
the lake. Then suddenly he was in a room with
the woman. She was cooking. The man read a
book. Neither of them looked at him or spoke

to him. Feeling invisible, he'd climbed wooden stairs to a stuffy room and closed the door—and woken up.

He rubbed his eyes, trying to clear the loneliness of the dream from his head. What was worse? Owls and screams or emptiness?

The mattress moved and he glanced down. Paige's arm was draped over his chest, and in the light coming through the curtains, he could just ascertain a sparkle in her eyes.

She inched closer, her fragrant hair spilling against his shoulder. "Are you okay?" she whispered.

"Don't tell me I was thrashing around or talking in my sleep," he said with dread.

"No," she assured him. "But it was kind of a rough day."

"Yeah," he said, gathering her in his arms. He relished the feel of her bare skin pressed against his. "It was tough, but I'm okay. Now."

"It's just sometimes when you wake up—"

"Not this time."

"Oh, that's good," she said as she slipped one of her silky, luscious legs over his hips. Her fingers caressed his backside in a wonderful, sensual way. "It seems a shame to waste this gaudy bed, doesn't it?" she added.

He touched her breast, wrapping his hand around the gentle curve, loving the weight of it and the texture, the way his thumb running over her nipple brought an immediate response. And not just from her. His own body was on fire, too.

"Ooh, I can see you share the sentiment," she whispered against his ear.

"We did pay extra for the heart," he murmured.

"I know. That's just what I thought."

"And I believe I gave you a rain check on the airplane," he added, pulling her even closer as his legs tangled with hers and her belly pressed against his excitement.

She sighed softly, her mouth against his neck now, the tip of her tongue soft and moist against his skin. "Yes, and I intend to collect right now."

THE OWLS WERE THERE AGAIN, swooping low over his head. He began to run, faster and faster, his feet pounding the ground. He had a flashlight and he held it aloft to shine at the owls, to frighten them away.

They each had the face of a child—

He awoke outside the hotel, standing on the sidewalk, out of breath. The doorman was staring at him and asked a question John couldn't understand above the fading call of the owls.

He shook his head and looked around. It appeared to be very early in the morning and he was standing there in nothing but his boxers.

It was freezing cold and raining, and he wasn't sure what to do.

The doorman, who appeared to be damn near unflappable, took a rain slicker from over his uniform and handed it to John with raised eyebrows. John shrugged it on, nodded his thanks and walked back into the hotel.

The front-desk crew stared at him, their startled expressions making it clear they'd witnessed him running through the lobby moments earlier. He directed a nod at them and tried to look as normal as possible as he went to the elevator and got inside.

He was turning into a damn freak show.

The room door was open. Paige was still asleep in the heart-shaped bed, long limbs tangled in pink satin sheets. He thought of crawling back into bed and waking her. Instead he took a shower and ordered breakfast from room service.

She awoke as the aroma of coffee and toast filled the room, and they ate breakfast sitting on the bed. He didn't tell her what had happened. He didn't know how.

Three hours later they arrived at the airport, and by then Paige had grown kind of thoughtful. John suspected she was worried about being out of touch with her family. He had to admit her mother and sister appeared to be on the flighty side. Paige had some of the same characteristics, however. She wouldn't have gone on this crazy trip with him if she didn't.

Was it possible Irina's mother was right, that the people he'd thought were his grandparents weren't? Was the first dream he'd had last night trying to tell him something? Was it really a reflection of what life with them had been like, or was it just a dream? And where did any of this leave him now?

And don't even start with the owls.

Irina believed Sergi and Galina were murdered. If they weren't murdered then they killed each other or themselves—who knew? Murder or suicide, was it just happenstance that it occurred on the same day he'd paid them a visit? Had he gone to see anyone else while he was in Kanistan a few weeks ago? And who had the Ognevas called after he left Slovo and before their deaths?

Dead ends. One after the other, and still not a concrete memory he could claim.

Paige's car was right where they left it in long-term parking, and as John went over the undercarriage making sure it wasn't fitted with another tracking device, she walked around in circles, fooling around on her phone as she paced.

It was obvious she'd reached somebody when

she started talking, but the call didn't last long. "That was my mother," she said as she rejoined him. He unlocked the trunk and she set the suitcase in the back as John retrieved his gun and holster and put them on under his jacket. Then she grabbed her laptop from the heap.

"How is she?"

"She broke up with what's-his-name."

"Has she heard from your sister?"

"I don't think so. She was crying so hard I couldn't understand her."

"It was a short call," he said, smoothing her hair away from her face.

"That's because she got an incoming from the ex-fiancé while we were talking. She had to take it. I give up. On to other things," Paige said as she slipped behind the wheel. "We need to get someplace where there's internet. It seems we've been out of touch for two weeks instead of two days."

He nodded, too caught up in thought to offer anything more.

What did he do now? Where did he go? Maybe it was time to turn himself in to the police and get some decent help. Maybe with what he and Paige knew about Anatola Korenev, the authorities could apprehend him.

"Aren't you curious if you're still wanted for murder?" she asked.

John grunted in a distracted manner as he stretched out his long legs and drummed his fingers against the armrest. His mind was racing.

"Are you worried the Ognevas aren't your grandparents?" she asked with a sideways glance.

"What?" He looked at her and shook his head. "Sorry. No, I don't remember them, but I have a feeling we weren't close anyway. Think about it. I left as soon as I was old enough and never went back until the day they happened to die.

"Anyway, when my memory returns, I'll go back to Kanistan and I'll find out more about them and about myself. That must be why I went the first time, and I'm betting it was something my aunt told me that connected a few dots. I'll connect them again. The bottom line is it's time to admit I need help. Looks like I'd better find a shrink."

"If you find a shrink and you're still wanted for murder, won't he or she have to turn you in?"

"I'm not sure."

She pulled over and guided the car into a hotel parking lot and got out her laptop, plugging the adapter into the cigarette lighter to boot it up. "Before you give up, let's just see where things stand," she said.

"While you're on there, search psychiatric ethics on Google. Can't hurt to be prepared."

She cast him a wry smile, then spent the next few minutes surfing the web. At last she whistled. "They reported this morning that John Cinca is now listed as a possible victim of a man known as Anatola Korenev. They mention Korenev's fingerprints were at the murder scenes and several other related sites of violence, including Cinca's residence. Oh, look, someone helped the police make a composite sketch. It's hard to see his face under all that hair." She turned the computer toward John. "What do you think?"

"They caught his glower," John said.

"The good news is you're not wanted for murder," Paige added.

"That is good news." As he sometimes did, he wondered if there was anyone important in his life who was grieving his supposed death right now.

"How about the guy in the coma?" he added. "Have they released his identity yet? Come to think of it, he's my last chance to find out something about myself. If he was there, he has to know something about me."

"Natalie said you were on a job. I can't believe you'd drive off with Korenev. You'd just been to Kanistan, so you'd recognize the accent."

"I kind of did, you know? I mean, at the cabin,

the first time he barged in and spoke, his accent seemed familiar but I didn't know why."

"I bet the guy in the coma is the one who hired you."

"And if he hired me or set me up or something, then maybe he knows why. I wonder if they've identified him yet."

"I'll look."

She did and a minute later folded the computer cover down. "They did identify him. His name is Chuck Miner. He's in a hospital in Green Acre, Wyoming, and his condition has been upgraded."

"Is he conscious?"

"The report was several hours old and they didn't say. It sounds as though he's got a record a mile long, though."

"Another crook? Man, I know how to pick my friends and associates, don't I?"

"Apparently," she said around a yawn. "Sorry," she added, smiling that way she had that made him want to find a room—with or without a heart-shaped bed. "I didn't get much sleep last night. There were all these…distractions."

He leaned across the seat and kissed her. "How about I drive to Green Acre and you catch forty winks. I want to know if Chuck Miner can have visitors."

"You got it," she said, but before he could move away, she'd wrapped her hand around the back of his neck and pulled him toward her again until their lips met.

Each kiss was as sweet as the first...so why did he keep feeling each might be the last?

PAIGE WOKE UP WHEN HER phone rang. As it was on her lap, she was able to glance at the caller ID before answering. "Katy. Thank goodness it's you."

"But it isn't her, is it?" came the reply.

A cold sweat broke out on Paige's forehead. Korenev had Katy's phone! "What have you done to her?"

"Did you and Cinca enjoy little trip to Kanistan? Shame you didn't wait until summer. Much warmer then. He should have warned you."

"Where is Katy?"

The tone of her voice had attracted John's attention. He pulled the car to the side of the road and turned in the seat to face her.

"Do you know where new apartment is?"

"Yes."

"There be a surprise there for you. Tell Mr. Cinca I will call. And don't contact police, not if you want to see sister again."

With that the phone went dead.

"Was it him?" John said as Paige lowered the phone.

She nodded, her throat too swollen to speak.

"What is it, Paige? What did he say? Is Katy okay?"

"I don't know," she blurted out. "He just said he had her. Oh my God, that monster has Katy."

John hit the steering wheel with his hand. "How—"

"I don't know any details. He knew we were in Kanistan, though. He says he's going to call you. I've been asleep. How far are we from Parker? He said we should go to her new apartment, that there was a surprise awaiting us there."

John immediately put the car in gear and got back on the road.

"Oh, John. I should have stayed with her."

"You are not at fault," John said firmly. "I am. I allowed this to keep going."

He was driving fast and he was obviously good at it. Of course he was, he'd been a cop for years. They were trained for things like high-speed driving.

"Call the police," John said. "Tell them about this. Get them over there."

"I can't," she said, voice trembling. "He said not to."

She dug in her purse for a tissue to wipe at

the tears that kept filling her eyes. "Go faster," she whispered, and he must have heard because his speed increased.

All she could think of was the time she'd spent with Korenev and the unmitigated fear she'd experienced in the face of his ruthless brutality. Now it was days later, he must know the police were after him and he'd been thwarted repeatedly. Who knew how angry he was now and what he would do in retaliation?

As they neared town, Paige started giving directions. She'd been to the Palms only once before, and that was to visit a college friend ten years before.

"Turn here," she said, then a minute later, "There it is, the green building. There's no parking lot. Hurry, just let me out while you go find a space."

He shook his head. "No way. We stay together."

A block down, he found street parking and they ran back to the apartment.

But which unit?

"Check the mailboxes," John said as he rang the bell on the central door, hoping someone would let them in. Paige's hands shook as she ran her fingers over the nameplates. Most looked as though they'd been there for years, but a white piece of paper with handwritten letters caught her eye. "Here it is, K. Graham. Apartment Nineteen. Let's go."

"We can't get in the—" He stopped talking as someone finally buzzed them in. John pushed the door open. A sign on the opposing wall of the small lobby area pointed at the stairs for apartments twelve through twenty. John grabbed her hand and they ran up the stairs together and then down the long hall.

Number nineteen was the last door on the north side of the building. "I'll break it down—" John started, but Paige tried the knob and the door opened.

There were boxes and furniture stacked everywhere. It didn't appear anything had been unpacked or arranged except Katy's portable TV, which had been set on the bar separating kitchen from living area. A bawdy comedy was currently playing with the volume turned up. A few empty water bottles and a couple of beer cans lay on the Formica countertop nearby as though people had paused during moving to catch their breath.

Despite the noise of the television, the room had an empty feel to it. Why had Korenev sent them here? What was the surprise he'd mentioned? And most important, where was Katy?

And then a sixth sense set in and Paige's skin began to crawl. She'd encountered the aura in this apartment before today and recently, too. The cloying odor...

"Paige, go out into the hall, please," John said, reaching for her arm, but she shrugged away, galvanized by the compulsion to move forward into the room. John couldn't protect her, he couldn't save her from this, and she knew it. She climbed over boxes as the characters in the show hurled insults at each other. And then she spied the edge of Katy's love seat and a scrap of yellow fabric.

She forced herself to continue moving, shoving aside a box spring that blocked her view.

A man wearing a yellow T-shirt and jeans lay sprawled across the pale gray leather, eyes open, a hole in his forehead, his hands clutching something wispy and brown.

Matt...

Canned laughter rang out in the background, then applause.

"Oh, no," John said, coming up behind her and gripping her arms. "Oh, damn. Poor kid." Releasing her, he moved to bend over the body and then straightened and shook his head as he met Paige's gaze.

The phone rang.

John held out his hand but Paige shook her head as she clicked it on and raised it to her ear. "Cinca?"

"No. You bastard—"

"Put Cinca on line."

"Where are you? Where's my sister? If you've hurt her—"

"Paige!" Katy yelled in the background and then Paige heard the unmistakable sound of a hard slap and the desperate cries that followed. Her own cheek stung as her stomach roiled in protest.

"This is not game," Korenev said. "Put Cinca on phone or sister end up like boy."

Paige handed the phone to John, bowing her head, but not before once again glimpsing Matt's sightless eyes.

As JOHN TOOK THE CELL, he watched Paige more or less stumble toward the hallway door, one hand clutching her stomach.

"Do you kill people just for the hell of it, is that it?" John barked into the phone.

"I do nothing just for hell of it. You have proved to be big pain."

"How did you know we went to Kanistan?"

"How can *you* ask such stupid question?" he replied. "Although why you go is mystery. Did you have nice talk with police?"

Korenev knew what they'd done in Kanistan. That raised all sorts of questions. None of that was important right now.

"You should have left things alone," Kore-nev said. "You be big liability. To get girl back, we trade. You for her. Simple. All this killing for nothing."

"What about the old guy in the fire truck? Why did you kill him?"

"Liability. He see me at warehouse. Had to go."

John kneaded his forehead a couple of times. "The police know your name," he said. "You won't be able to leave the country. If you release Katy—"

"Oh, come now. We both know I not give real name. Even fingerprints won't find the real me. Even silly drawing of hairy man. Now listen to me. I say once. Go to rural airport located outside city of Cheyenne. You know it?"

"I can find it."

"Both of you come. When you get there, you wait by south fence. I will watch to make sure you do not bring police or make trap. Then we exchange."

"That has to be a good three hours from here," John said. He glimpsed Paige's desperate expression and wondered how she would make it three more hours.

"Then go. Sister depending on you." And with that he disconnected.

"We're going to Cheyenne," John said, joining Paige at the door.

"What about Matt?"

They were leaving a depressing trail of bodies in their wake, but this situation was the same as the others. Matt had been dead for hours if not a day or so. "If we call the cops, they'll want to get in on the swap and Korenev said—"

"I can guess what he said. You're right, we can't call them." She looked back into the room, her eyes moist and unbearably sad. "Could we cover Matt's body?"

"Better not," John said. "Best to leave the scene as it is."

"Then I'm at least going to turn off that stupid television," she said, and although he started to protest, it was obvious she had to do something for her fallen friend. He'd tuned out the noise a while before, but now it came back loud and clear.

She walked into the room and reached for the remote, then paused.

The police drawing of Korenev filled the screen with contact numbers scrolling across the top. The picture switched to a bronzed newscaster. "As previously reported," he said into the camera, "one of Korenev's first known victims, Chuck Miner, has regained consciousness. Police are hopeful Miner will be able to shed light on a recent slew of killings that has taken the lives of at least three people in Wyoming. They plan an interview tomorrow morning. Tune in at six for details."

Paige clicked off the television. The sudden silence was deafening.

"Come on, honey," John said, his voice low. "We'll get Katy back, I promise, then this will be over." She nodded. He couldn't tell if she believed him or not. He knew he sure as hell didn't.

It just didn't seem as if it would ever be over.

They locked the door behind them.

Chapter Fourteen

Paige let John drive. Between Matt's face and Katy's scream, her mind was too filled with horror to concentrate on traffic.

Was there a time in the past few days where if things had been done differently, if she'd behaved differently, the people in her life would not be dead or in jeopardy?

The answer was yes.

Whatever John had started in motion before he met her was beyond her to change, but it was her fault Korenev had come into *her* life.

But that wasn't true. What about the Pollocks?

So, maybe the question was, did things make sense at the time? Did decisions make sense when they were made? And she didn't know the answer for sure, but her gut was tortured with the speculation that Matt's death and Katy's abduction were her fault.

She sneaked a peek at John. From the expres-

;ion on his face, she'd wager he was drawing the very same conclusion about his own conduct.

And now a guy named Miner was conscious, and it must be killing John to drive the other direction.

"What did you mean when you said we were going to swap?" she asked. "Swap what?"

He'd obviously been deep in thought because it took him a few seconds to respond.

"Katy for me," he said, not looking at her.

"What? Are you nuts? He'll kill both of you."

"No," he said, "I won't let him hurt her."

"This is suicide."

"I have three hours to think of a plan. I'll come up with something."

She put her hand on his thigh and he finally glanced at her. "I'm sorry you aren't on your way to talk to Miner. I know speaking with him meant a lot to you."

"First things first," he said succinctly. "Katy is the priority now."

"She's my only sister and I know she's a screwball, but it doesn't matter. I can't help but feel this is all my fault."

"You don't have to explain anything about guilt to me," he said. "I take full responsibility for this whole mess."

"Don't flatter yourself," she said. "You had plenty of help. Korenev has done his best to destroy everything and everyone he comes across."

He spared her a longer look, then concentrated on driving again. "I just wish that somewhere along the line I'd gotten a few answers instead of new questions. And I wish I had more time with you."

"Wait a second," she said. "That sounds an awful lot like a goodbye. Don't do that to me."

He covered her hand with his, but he didn't look at her.

She felt her eyes water again and she blinked it away. "Korenev has eliminated or tried to eliminate everyone who got a glimpse of his undisguised face," she said. "I sure hope he didn't let Katy see him."

John took his foot off the accelerator so suddenly the car behind them honked as it swerved past.

"John! What's wrong?"

He shook his head, but at least he sped up again. Only for a while, though. They were just leaving Parker on their way to the freeway, but he pulled over to the curb instead of taking the ramp. He turned in the seat and stared at her.

"What is it?" she repeated.

"What you just said about Korenev eliminating the people who saw his face. That's why he killed Jack Pollock. And then he went inside to make sure the wife was dead, too, because maybe she'd seen him through a window or something. That's why he was going to kill you. It's why he took out the old guy in the fire truck and Matt, too. Did you see the long, dark hairs caught in Matt's fingers?"

"I saw something brown."

"Matt must have grabbed at Korenev's fake beard or wig. I bet Katy saw his face, as well. This trip to Cheyenne is a farce, a diversion. We have to turn around."

"What? No. We have to get Katy."

"Katy isn't in Cheyenne any more than Korenev is. He knows about Miner waking up. That news clip said 'as previously reported.' In other words, it had already been aired, so Korenev knew about it when he called."

"How do we know he watches TV or listens to a radio or—"

"Because he does. He knew about the composite sketch made of him. He's no idiot. He also knew exactly when we entered Katy's apartment. He gave us less then five minutes before calling, and he didn't ask if we were there yet or anything, did he?"

"No."

"Because he knew. He was close by and he knew we were there. So he sends us off to Cheyenne while he does the most logical thing—for him."

"Which is what?" she said. "Can't we drive toward Cheyenne while we talk?"

"Korenev is not in Cheyenne. He's on his way to Green Acre to take care of Miner, the last loose end, besides Katy and me. And you, Paige. You, too."

"No," she said firmly. "He told you to go to Cheyenne because for some unexplained reason, getting rid of you is his major goal. He won't jeopardize an opportunity to get rid of all three of us in one fell swoop just because of Chuck Miner."

"Yes, he will. It's precisely because he has Katy that he can call the shots. Until he gets his hands on me or you, she's safe. And I'm telling you, she's not in Cheyenne. You heard her call out your name, right, and him silence her? Even I heard that. She's with him and he's on his way to Green Acre, which is where we're going, too."

"No," she cried as he made a U-turn. "Absolutely not. I forbid it. The man is a murderer. We have to rescue Katy."

He pulled the car to the opposite curb. "Paige. Trust me one more time."

"No," she said. She was not backing down. She'd been selfish, she'd been blinded by her feelings, but no more. She was too late for Matt, but Katy was still alive. "No," she said, tears running down her face now. "I can't."

He sat back as though stunned by her objection. "We don't have time for this," he said.

"Then drive to Cheyenne."

He took a deep breath. "Paige, listen—"

"No." She gathered her thoughts. Her hands shook, her voice quavered. "John, I think it's possible you've never had a family or really loved anyone or been responsible for them in such an organic way that it's built into your DNA. Maybe that's one of those closed doors Natalie sensed about you. But my crazy family is part of me and I cannot, I will not, abandon them on a whim and a hope."

He shook his head.

"If Korenev sees me in Cheyenne without you," she added, "he'll just kill Katy and me both. You're willing to walk away knowing that?"

Now his voice shook, too. "I'm not walking away. I'm heading a different direction because it's the only way to save you and Katy. Can't you see that? Come with me."

"And can't you see that you're off on another wild-goose chase? You want to know your past so badly you're willing to abandon good sense."

"I can't believe you think that of me," he said.

"And I can't believe I allowed myself to love

a man who would abandon me when I needed him most. What am I supposed to think?"

He stared hard at her a minute. "Then this is where we finally say goodbye," he said, his voice cracking. "I'll go my way and you go yours. I want you to take the gun—just in case. Don't argue with me. Just point it and pull the trigger if you have to."

"If you're so sure about this, then why are you giving me your gun?" she asked.

It took him a moment to answer. "Because I love you, too," he finally said.

Lips trembling, Paige turned her face away.

IN THE END, THEY FOUND a car rental place and Paige, being the only one with a valid driver's license and a credit card, rented another vehicle. Within ten minutes, she drove away in the rental with a few of her belongings as John took off in the other direction in her car.

He'd told her about the south fence at the Cheyenne airport and how she was just supposed to sit there until Korenev called on her cell. It would be dark by then, but there wasn't a doubt in her mind that Korenev would know she'd come alone before he made that call and he would suspect a trick, or worse, just shoot her and Katy and go after John again.

John had always come through when it

counted, so how could he have left now? His betrayal scorched her heart way worse than Brian's had. It reached deeper and tapped into things darker. More than once, she flipped tears from her cheeks as the traffic around her blurred.

She'd started to believe in him— No, wait, she'd believed in him from the very start. Even with the quirks and nightmares and mounting evidence of corruption, she'd known on an internal level who and what he was.

Or had she?

She couldn't bear to think of him, but that opened her mind to images of Katy, bound with duct tape and stuck in the trunk of some old car. Paige knew firsthand how frightening Korenev could be with his icy eyes and cold steel blade, with his cavalier brutality. And Katy was way more delicate than Paige, more protected. She must be terrified.

The phone rang as it began to rain. *John, please, please, be John calling to say you've changed your mind.* No matter how tenuous their future was at this point, Katy needed him. She needed him.

She knew she shouldn't answer the phone while driving, especially in an unfamiliar car, but she did it anyway. "Yes?"

"Paige," a man said.

"Yes? Who is this?"

"Paige, darling, don't you recognize my voice?"

And suddenly she did. "Brian? What do you want? Why are you calling? Is something wrong?"

"I guess it depends on how you look at it," he said.

What did that mean? "Is Jasmine okay?"

"I don't know," he said. "She left."

Paige stared at the bus traveling in front of her and tried to make sense of Brian's words. "Where'd she go?"

"She got a lot of media attention after the attack. There were interviews and some went national. Well, you probably saw them. She was everywhere for a day or so. She just loved the attention and the camera loved her. She got an offer to audition for a reality show so she flew off to L.A. She's not coming back no matter what. She's gone."

Almost speechless, Paige managed a subdued, "I'm sorry."

"Maybe it's for the best," he said. "Things haven't been so good between us lately. Damn it, Paige, the truth is I knew the day after I went back to her that I'd made a terrible mistake."

Paige literally did not know how to respond.

"Seeing you the other day with another guy was like a pail of cold water in my face. I've screwed up big-time, Paige, I know that, but what we had was good. I'm asking you to give me another chance."

After several seconds of silence, Paige finally managed to speak. "This isn't a good time for me."

"No, don't say that," he begged. "Please don't say that, darling. Listen to me. When Jasmine showed up at our wedding and wanted me back it was like the planet fell back into orbit. But in the end, I just hurt you and myself, too, and now I want to fix it. Just tell me you'll give us a chance. Think about what we had. We can have it again."

Hadn't Paige felt that exact way when she saw him? Everything had seemed perfect for a moment and she'd been ready to sell her soul just to have back what had been taken away from her. How big a hypocrite would she be not to understand how Brian could have felt the same way?

But his timing really was terrible.

JOHN STRUGGLED TO PUT Paige out of his mind, but the way she hadn't been able even to look him in the eyes when they parted seemed to have lodged somewhere in his chest. If he was wrong about Korenev, Paige might very well pay for it with her life. That thought alone was enough to consider turning around. Perhaps they should just face whatever happened next together. Together—that was the key word.

But that word no longer described them and he seriously doubted it ever would again. Besides, he didn't think he was wrong, and if he was right, not only would Paige be safe and sound hundreds of miles away from the inevitable carnage, but he would save her sister. That was what mattered: saving Katy. Otherwise Paige would carry the unwarranted guilt of her sister's fate for the rest of her life.

So he kept driving Paige's car, her presence so real he could almost see her sitting beside him, her absence even more real.

As sunlight faded into evening shadows, he drove into Green Acre, a picturesque town with a distinct Western flair. He passed a metal sculpture of a moose and another of a bear as Paige's GPS directed him to the hospital.

As he drove through the ever-darkening parking lot, he kept his eyes peeled for a battered van but didn't see one. That didn't mean much, as Korenev had undoubtedly traded in that vehicle for another. The man treated the world like a giant used-car lot.

Which raised the question: Where was Katy? She was obviously with Korenev, or had been when he called them at Katy's apartment. If Korenev was already here, that probably meant

Katy was close by, but where? Korenev wouldn't have taken her into the hospital with him, but he could have dumped her anywhere along the way or stuck her in a trunk and parked almost anywhere in this town. John looked over the sea of cars and knew he didn't have time to investigate each of them.

First things first. He'd start by checking out the hospital.

The building was undergoing major renovation and John passed signs apologizing for the inconvenience almost every place he turned. Patient rooms were on the second floor so he took the elevator, sharing the ride with a couple of orderlies and a cart of covered meal trays. Apparently it was dinner hour.

The small alcove with a centralized nursing station was unmanned when John got there and he stood around for a few minutes, anxious beyond endurance but unsure how to proceed. Monitors behind the counter obviously reflected the vital signs of various patients, but they were labeled with room numbers, not names and so, were of no help.

A team of workers plied their trade nearby, making a heck of a racket as they wielded drills and hammers. John was about one second away from jumping over the counter and trying his hand with the computer to find Miner when a plump woman carrying a stack of folders finally appeared from behind a sheet of thick plastic that hung across the hallway. She sidestepped the workmen and quickened her pace when she saw John.

"I'm sorry," she said. "I hope you haven't been waiting long. Half the staff is out with the flu and this construction is driving the rest of us nuts. How can I help you?"

"Miner?" John asked.

"Charles Miner? Chuck?"

Charles? John narrowed his eyes, the name resonating in his head. He'd never made the leap from Chuck to Charles and it wasn't an issue right now, but his aunt had called him Charles.

"Room 220," she added. "I'm not sure he's allowed visitors. Check with the guard outside his room. Down the hall on the left. Just be cautious of the uneven floor, please. Turn right and go straight past the stairway. Wait, I think Mr. Miner was having some tests. Oh, you'll find out when you get there."

"Has he had any other visitors today?" John asked.

"I don't think so. Like I said, we've been in and out of his room." The nurse turned back to what she was doing and John took off down the hall, his heart hammering inside his chest. He wouldn't put anything past Korenev, and with all the chaos and inattention abounding in the hospital, who knew where he was or even what he currently looked like?

Halfway down the corridor, John came across an empty metal chair by the door of room 220. There were two women standing farther down the hall, but neither wore a police or security-officer uniform.

So where was the guard? Out of habit, John patted himself to check for his gun before recalling he'd forced Paige to take it.

As he paused, uncertain how to proceed, the door of room 220 opened inward and three people in lab coats exited. One rolled a cart covered with glass vials of what appeared to be blood samples. The other two were laden with stethoscopes, clipboards and medical paraphernalia John didn't recognize, although he didn't actually stand there staring at them. Instead, he walked on down the hall, pausing in front of a closet marked Supplies, straining to listen to the conversation among the people exiting Miner's room.

"Hey, where's the guard?" the woman rolling the cart said. The cart made an amazing amount of noise on the uneven floor as its contents rattled together.

A man with a deep voice responded. "Must have taken a coffee break."

"I'll be glad when this construction is over," the third person said as they continued down the hall, their voices fading. John saw his big chance, but knew it probably wouldn't last long. He retraced his steps in a hurry and let himself into the room, closing the door behind him.

He came face-to-face with a curtain and hesitated again. It shielded whoever was in the room from view when the door was open, so it would provide him cover once he was behind it. On the other hand, it would also obscure the identity of any newcomer. Better to have no surprises. He silently pushed the curtain aside.

Chuck Miner looked to be in his mid-thirties, though with all the cuts, bruises and bandages, it was hard to be certain. He also appeared to be asleep, which seemed amazing considering how many people had just left his room.

John's nerves were raw with tension. Everything looked so normal. My God, what if he was wrong about Korenev? That would mean he'd sent Paige off into chaos. He reached for his cell as he quietly walked to the window. He'd been so sure he was right.

She didn't answer. She always answered. She hadn't had time to get all the way to Cheyenne, and he had the sickening feeling she wasn't responding because she saw the call was from him....

He stared down at the well-lit lot for a second as the phone switched to her voice mail. Was it possible Korenev had seen John enter the hospital and was now waiting for him to come back out? Hell and damnation, anything was possible.

Chuck-Charles. The name came back again, as elusive as a web of invisible thread. That's what his aunt had called him. She'd thought he was Charles.

His father.

For a second, John stopped breathing. His father was named Charles, he was sure of it although he wasn't sure how.

Suddenly a flock of large, dark birds appeared out of nowhere and swooped over a nearby lamppost, veering toward the hospital window right at John. John gasped, threw his hands over his head and backed up, dropping the phone in the process. For a second, he cowered, and then he straightened up and braced his hands on the window frame, peering outside, scanning the darkening sky.

Nothing.

But he'd seen them, and now their sounds filled his head. In a parody of his nightmares, the hooting morphed into screams, and these pierced him like poison darts.

Owls swooping in the night, chasing him, children screaming.

Children screaming…

He was screaming.

But he wasn't, it was all in his head. Everything was in his head. Without a single doubt, he *knew* that the same overwhelming guilt that currently churned his gut with agonizing worry about Paige and her sister was familiar—it had happened to him before. He'd been responsible before, responsible for something that had ended in disaster.

But what?

His fault…

He had to get out of this room. He had to find Korenev and Katy. He had to find Paige.

He swallowed hard and turned from the window.

Chuck Miner stared at him with confused pale eyes in which enlightenment dawned like the lighting of a match. He pointed at John. "I thought you were dead," he said.

"Tell me how we met before," John said. His voice sounded scratchy, as though bird talons had clawed their way up his throat.

Miner narrowed his eyes. "I know I set you up, but you gotta believe me, I didn't know he was going to try to kill you."

"You hired me, didn't you?" John said. He was trying hard to hear Miner over the screams in his own brain.

"Sure. I gave you some song and dance about an old girlfriend blackmailing me and you fell for it. Listen, you gotta believe me, that guy Korenev said he just wanted to rough you up a little, and all I had to do was hire you for some made-up job and get you up to that park and then get lost for a while. But you know how it went down. You and I drove up together, then Korenev attacked both of us and you disappeared into the river. What did you ever do to that guy?"

"I'm not sure," John said. "Where is he now, do you know? How did you get in contact with him before? I have to find him—"

Miner held up his hands. "I don't know, man. I never called him, he called me. I never want to see that dude again."

The phantom screams had actually grown louder. Damn, he didn't have time for head games. "I have to go."

"Say, why are you here?" Miner asked.

"I'm not sure," John said, swallowing hard. He took a step, amazed at how the floor seemed to buckle under his feet. Stumbling, he grabbed the back of a chair to steady himself.

"What's wrong with you?" Miner demanded.

Good question. John took a deep breath. "Korenev will try to get to you," he said. "You need to…to get the guard back on your door."

Miner's gaze shifted that direction and back. "What? The nurses who were in here before said he was out there."

"He wasn't when I came into the room."

And right on cue, there was a noise at the door and both Miner and John turned to look. If it was the guard checking in, he'd demand to know what John was doing here, and John wasn't sure he could explain. He didn't have time for this. He had to get to Cheyenne, and it was hours away.

Paige.

A gray-haired orderly wearing Coke-bottle glasses and green hospital scrubs juggled a dinner tray with his left hand as he closed the door behind him.

John took another deep breath. He couldn't seem to get enough air.

The orderly's nearsighted gaze darted between Miner and John as he slowly approached the bed and set the tray on the rolling table. His hand caught John's attention as the light reflected on a gold-and-black ring.

Miner pushed the tray away. "Was the guard out there?" he asked the orderly.

The orderly shook his head.

"Call someone for me, get the guard back," Miner pleaded. "And take the food away, I'm not hungry."

Silently, the orderly picked up the tray and, in one sudden and violent sweep of his arm, swung it at Miner, hitting him in the head with it. Miner slumped unconscious. Lime Jell-O ran down his face.

But the signet ring was all that John could really see. A gold-embossed owl set on a jet oval. It was as though dynamite exploded in his brain. He gripped his head. His skin was on fire. He knew that ring.

The orderly removed the glasses from his face. In an instant, he turned into Anatola Korenev—or whoever he really was. A knife appeared next, held in his maimed right hand. With a backward stabbing motion, he speared Miner without his gaze straying from John's face.

"Your turn next, Mr. Cinca," he said with no emotion as he wiped the blade clean on the bedsheet.

Chapter Fifteen

"Where's Katy?" John said, but it sounded like a squeak. He was only half-aware of the blood blossoming across Miner's chest. He could not take his eyes off that ring. The room seemed to swirl like a whirlpool with the golden owl the center of the disturbance, the eye of the hurricane, sucking him in.

"Sister is dead," Korenev said, advancing with a limp. "Paige Graham next, after you."

He'd failed. He'd been right and wrong at the same time, and he'd failed. Paige would suffer because of him if she didn't manage to avoid Korenev—or even if she did. "Who are you?" John asked. "Why are you doing this?"

"Real name Aleksey Smirnov. Head of security in Traterg. Ring bells? No? You think we don't know you come to Kanistan last month to ask questions of Ognevas? They call us."

"And you killed them. Who were they?"

He shrugged. "Just people. They had job to do, that is all. What did they tell you?"

"I don't know, I don't remember," John said.

"Doesn't matter now. You get back memory of being boy, you have to die."

Being boy. "The ring—"

"See, is true. I forget to take off ring."

"There was an explosion."

"Meant for ambassador."

Ambassador! "I don't understand."

"Too much talk, I lose time in hallway closet with dead guard waiting for medic people to leave. Then here you are, too, like big gift. If I had my way, you would be dead years and years ago when you were nosy boy in wrong place at wrong time."

John had kept retreating as they spoke. Images were bombarding his head, images at once vague and yet vivid, more vivid even than what was unfolding in this room, in front of his eyes. It was the same ring, but it was on the hand of a clown and it held a box.

And then an explosion. *Tyler! Cole!*

Brothers. They were his brothers….

"What did you do to them? To Tyler and Cole?"

"Dead," Korenev said. "You see them soon."

John finally backed into the wall. In a flash, Korenev was upon him, transferring the knife into his left hand so that now it was the owl that gripped the handle. Reality crashed back in a searing streak of pain as the glinting blade slid into John's stomach.

John gasped and began to sag. He knew Korenev would hold on to the knife while gravity pulled John to the floor, gutting him like a fish.

He heard a shot.

Korenev, shock written on his face, gray wig askew, managed a halfway turn before collapsing.

With both hands, John gripped the knife handle that protruded from his gut. He looked across the room. An angel stood at the open door, holding a gun straight out in front of her.

"Paige," he whispered as the world shrank to a single black dot.

PAIGE DROPPED THE GUN, screamed for help, then ran to John. She cradled his head, paralyzed with fear. She was too late.

"Hold on," she pleaded. There was very little blood; perhaps the knife more or less plugged the hole in his body. She smoothed his damp forehead. He was very pale.

"I love you, John. Please don't leave me," she whispered as she smoothed his forehead. She'd remembered that twenty seconds after hanging up from Brian. Then she'd turned around and headed this direction, turning off her phone so Korenev couldn't call, or Brian, either. One thought had consumed her—go to John. Right or wrong, Katy or no Katy, her place was with him, and she did trust him, she'd always trusted him. Why stop now when the stakes were so high?

But where was Katy? She shouldn't have killed Korenev. She should have just wounded him and then beat Katy's whereabouts out of him. She'd reacted in blind panic when she saw what he was doing to John, but now how would she find Katy?

People arrived and the room was suddenly crowded. The bed was pushed aside, Paige was pulled to her feet. Tears rolled unheeded down her cheeks as they carefully lifted John onto a gurney. Would she ever see him alive again?

"Leave the others, they're both dead," someone said as they raced out of the room, wheeling John between them.

"Wait for me," Paige called, but a nurse turned and caught her arm.

"There's nothing you can do, honey. The waiting area is down the hall. Go there, the police will want to talk to you, as well as the hospital office. We'll need information on the injured man."

"But John—"

"He's going into surgery immediately. I'll let you know as soon as he's out."

She bustled off. Paige didn't want to go sit in a room and wait for bureaucracy to grind into gear, not when she was riddled with worry about John and with Katy still missing. She had to do something.

She turned around and stared at Korenev's corpse. He'd hot-wired cars in the past, but it was also possible he had stolen cars whose owners had left the keys in the ignition. It was worth a shot.

She immediately knelt down and tore through his clothes as she fought the revulsion of touching him. At last she found his keys. There were only three and none looked as though it belonged to a vehicle. She checked his other pocket just to make sure and hit pay dirt in the form of a key chain that held a single battered-looking key. The clincher was the tiny pink leather cowboy boot used as a fob—no way would Korenev own something like this.

She gripped it tight in her hand. Stepping over Korenev's body, she started for the door just as a whole new group of people began arriving. One tried to stop her, but Paige kept going, breaking into a run. She took the stairs instead of the elevator and burst out of the hospital only to stop dead in her tracks.

Police sirens in the distance warned her there wasn't much time until someone came looking for her. She ran to the rental and got in, then took off for the perimeter of the lot. She'd start on one side and circle around to the other, looking for an old vehicle parked off by itself where there were few lights.

And found it amazing how many old cars, trucks and vans tended to get parked by the fence. She got out of her car at each and every one of them, pounding on metal, peering in windows, yelling Katy's name, trying to fit Korenev's key in the door of the vans or the trunks of the cars.

What if he'd broken his pattern and taken a new vehicle or parked under a bright light? She should have asked everyone in that hospital to help. Why had she tried to do it by herself?

Fifteen vehicles later, her headlights swept over the bumper of an old white van and Paige hammered on the brakes. The bumper sticker was red and pink and said Cowgirls Do It on a Horse.

She got out of the rental with the engine still running, the headlights illuminating the double back doors. Heart in throat, Paige tried the key and sure enough, it slipped in the lock. With shaking hands, she turned it.

The interior consisted of a large open space

covered with cast-off hay. Bridles and halters and other horse tack hung on a rack affixed to the side walls. On top of the hay lay a pile of blankets. Paige started pulling at them.

A moment later she lifted the last one to uncover her sister's ashen face. "Oh, Katy," she murmured as she took in the cut on her left cheekbone, the swelling on her forehead, the silver duct tape covering her mouth and her closed eyes. She looked dead.

Climbing in the van next to her, Paige touched Katy's throat and felt the flutter of her pulse.

"What's going on out here?" a man's voice boomed.

Paige had been so focused on Katy that she hadn't heard anyone approach. She looked up now to see a large man in a uniform shining a flashlight on her.

"I got a report someone was going berserk out here, yelling and banging on cars," he added. His gaze dipped and his eyes widened. "Lordy, ma'am, what's wrong with her? Is she dead?"

"No, she's not dead. She's my sister and she was kidnapped," Paige explained. "Help me get her up to the hospital."

A few minutes later, with an unconscious Katy stretched out on the backseat and the hospital security officer following, Paige drove to the emergency-room door. The officer must have phoned ahead because the car was met by three people and a gurney and Katy was transferred inside.

Paige left the car where it was and followed. She called her mother, who had just learned about Matt's murder on the television, and promised to come at once. She gave insurance information and personal details about Katy to the hospital office, and then she ran upstairs.

Katy was safe. But what about John?

A Few Days Later:

"YOU CAN GO HOME TOMORROW if there's someone to help you out for a few days," the doctor said.

John looked at Paige, whose perfect lips curved in a suggestive smile. "I think I can squeeze you in," she said. "If there isn't a wife or a girlfriend—"

"Just you," John interrupted, and he knew it would always be just her. Always.

The doctor finished bandaging the wound and whistled as he walked toward the door. Pausing, he looked back. "How that knife missed every important organ is beyond me," he said. He tapped the wall with his hand and added, "You are a lucky man."

John knew he was a lucky man. He was alive, Paige was with him, Katy had left the hospital days before, Aleksey Smirnov, aka Anatola Korenev, was dead. And the icing on the cake?

He knew who he was in a way he hadn't since he was ten years old.

"I think I've heard everything, but in such bits and pieces that there are some things I'm confused about," Paige said, settling herself on the bed next to him. She crossed her long legs as she settled in, her hips by his head. He couldn't wait until he healed.

"So, explain."

"Which part?" he asked.

"Just start at the beginning and I'll stop you when I get bored."

"Well, let's see. My mother died when I was very young. She'd been sick for a while and one day she was just gone. My father remarried after a while, a woman named Mary."

"Did you like her?"

"I'm not sure. I think I did. I think I was also jealous because suddenly I had to share my dad. They had two little boys back-to-back and then Dad got appointed ambassador to Kanistan. We all moved there together. I was about nine or ten, Tyler was two or three and Cole was a year younger than him. We lived in a really neat house, I remember that."

"Where?"

"On the outskirts of Traterg. And things went

pretty well. Dad got friendly with one of his assistants and he and his wife came to the house once in a while, my stepmother joined all sorts of clubs, I liked having brothers and I didn't have to go to a real school, I got to have a tutor. There always seemed to be parties and stuff to do."

"Were you aware of the things Irina mentioned, you know, the border tensions and the police corruption and all that?"

She was absently running her fingers through his hair as they talked. He never wanted her to stop. "No, we were pretty sheltered."

"And then you said the circus came to town."

"That's right. We were all supposed to go, but Dad called in the afternoon and told my stepmother he had to work late and we should go without him. So we did. Right in the middle of the big show in the tent, Cole got sick and started throwing up so we had to come home. Tyler was crying and I thought it was totally unfair that a stupid baby ruined our good time. Nice, huh?"

"You were a kid."

"I know. Dad was home by then and he went to help my stepmother with Cole, and that's when the doorbell rang. Usually a servant answered it but they'd gotten the evening off because we were all going to be away from the house, so I went to the door."

"And saw a clown."

"And saw a clown. He seemed surprised to find me standing there. He was holding a box and I thought that somehow my stepmother or dad had arranged to have a treat delivered to me because Cole ruined everything. The clown said the box was for my father, and then he handed it to me and I saw the ring on his hand. A black oval with a gold owl. He left right away."

Talking about this for the third or fourth time was beginning to domesticate it in his mind. At first these memories had been like living with a tiger in the house, but now it was more like an unruly cat that came and went without too much fuss. Still, he knew he was talking faster and he knew his heart had sped up, but Paige's fingers were still touching his head, her strokes a little firmer now, as though she understood.

"I put the box on the table but it was too much. A clown had delivered it, I knew it was for me. So, I started to unwrap it. That's when Mary, my stepmother, came into the room and saw what I was doing. When I told her about the clown she seemed to think I'd made it up and she scolded me for touching something addressed to my father. I got furious with her.

I knew she never would have scolded Cole or Tyler. I told her I hated her."

"And your father heard?"

"Yes. He was livid. He scolded me, too, and I think I told him I hated him, as well, and then stomped off as they unwrapped the box. The next thing I knew, there was a horrible explosion, I was flying through the air, the babies were screaming....

"And then the pain, I was on fire...and then I was waking up and I didn't know who I was or what had happened to me. Nothing. A total blank."

She leaned down and kissed his forehead, his eyelids. "Oh, my poor darling. I think you felt so guilty because of the way everything happened that you couldn't bear to remember. It was too painful."

"I think you're right," he murmured. "I blamed myself."

"And made up your mind you didn't deserve to be loved because you were bad. You know now that's all wrong, don't you?"

"Just keep doing what you're doing," he said. "I'm catching on."

Her laugh was soft and thrilling and was followed by the touch of her lips on his. She was the best medicine in the world. God, how he loved her.

"You remember Irina told us about the ambassador and the bomb, right? She said the man was having an affair and the woman's family retaliated when he 'got rid' of her."

"I remember. But I don't believe it for a minute."

"Do you know how you ended up living with the Ognevas?"

"Not really. All I know was the Ognevas told me they were my grandparents, but it was obvious they couldn't stand the sight of me. It wasn't until my aunt contacted me years later that I learned the truth, that she'd been told we all died in that explosion. I learned that my father's family had disowned him when he refused to work the family business, which was worth millions. That's where all the money came from. Aunt Carol saw my picture in the paper. Apparently, I'm the spitting image of my father, her brother, Charles. She wanted to meet me, she wanted to know if it was possible I was her nephew and if I knew what happened to my brothers. And she told me she was dying and she wanted an heir, or three of them if I could find the other two. I wish I'd been able to tell her I did before she died a few days ago."

"And left you filthy rich. It must be nice to know you weren't a crooked cop, although I believe I told you so."

He pointed at his lips and she smiled as she kissed him again. "I know you did. From now on I'll believe every nice thing you say about me, no matter how unfounded," he whispered. "No, I didn't take bribes. Andy Patter, my partner, did. He and his wife adopted a baby and then the birth mother refused to sign the final papers unless he paid her. He took the bribes and gave the money to the woman. I got home from Canada to find he was under investigation, so I took the rap. The department let it go without pressing criminal charges to save face, and Andy and his family disappeared."

"You gave up your reputation."

"Better than him losing his baby. Besides, I had plenty of money thanks to my aunt and a new goal in life: find my brothers."

"So, you took off for Kanistan."

"Yes. I spoke with the Ognevas. I told them I knew they weren't my grandparents and demanded to know about the rest of my family. They said my parents died in the explosion but they weren't sure about the boys."

"Did you believe them?"

"At the time I wasn't sure. I decided to go to Traterg and find someone official to talk to, but I got a major runaround instead. My plane was leaving the next day so I decided to come home and go back after I did some investigation from this end. Someone forged my papers, someone changed my name from John Oates to John Cinca. Why? I didn't know the Ognevas called someone after I left or that the call got them killed, and I have no idea why."

"It seems as though someone didn't want them talking to you again."

"Exactly." He sighed deeply. "But I do know Aleksey Smirnov delivered the bomb to the house and that he was with the police. Why would anyone want to obliterate my family or even just my father? Did it have something to do with diplomacy or their border problems? That's what I have to find out."

"What about your brothers? Do you know if they survived?"

"No," he said slowly. "On the other hand, since getting back the early memories as well as the later ones, I have a memory of the bombing. The boys were off in the bedroom wing, I was relatively close by to the detonation. Plus, my last memory is of one or both of them screaming. If I survived, I think they must have survived, as well. I promise you this: I will find them and I will uncover what happened to my father and stepmother, or my name isn't John Oates."

"That's going to take some getting used to," she said.

"How about the name Paige Oates?" he asked and held his breath.

"Hmm—" she murmured. "Kind of has a nice ring to it, doesn't it?"

"I think so."

"Close your eyes," she said so softly her voice was like a memory, her touch as light as a sigh. "Go to sleep, my love."

They fell silent, and eventually her caresses coaxed him into unconsciousness.

And when he dreamed, it wasn't of owls.

* * * * *

Alice Sharpe's THE LEGACY *continues next month with* MONTANA REFUGE. *Look for it wherever Harlequin Intrigue books are sold!*

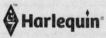

FAMOUS FAMILIES

YES! Please send me the *Famous Families* collection featuring the Fortunes, the Bravos, the McCabes and the Cavanaughs. This collection will begin with 3 FREE BOOKS and 2 FREE GIFTS in my very first shipment— and more valuable free gifts will follow! My books will arrive in 8 monthly shipments until I have the entire 51-book *Famous Families* collection. I will receive 2-3 free books in each shipment and I will pay just $4.49 U.S./$5.39 CDN for each of the other 4 books in each shipment, plus $2.99 for shipping and handling.* If I decide to keep the entire collection, I'll only have paid for 32 books because 19 books are free. I understand that accepting the 3 free books and gifts places me under no obligation to buy anything. I can always return a shipment and cancel at any time. My free books and gifts are mine to keep no matter what I decide.

268 HCN 0387   468 HCN 0387

Name _____ (PLEASE PRINT)

Address _____ Apt. #

City _____ State/Prov. _____ Zip/Postal Code

Signature (if under 18, a parent or guardian must sign)

Mail to the **Reader Service:**

IN U.S.A.: P.O. Box 1867, Buffalo, NY 14240-1867
IN CANADA: P.O. Box 609, Fort Erie, Ontario L2A 5X3

* Terms and prices subject to change without notice. Prices do not include applicable taxes. Sales tax applicable in N.Y. Canadian residents will be charged applicable taxes. This offer is limited to one order per household. All orders subject to approval. Credit or debit balances in a customer's account(s) may be offset by any other outstanding balance owed by or to the customer. Please allow 4 to 6 weeks for delivery. Offer available while quantities last. Offer not available to Quebec residents.

Your Privacy— The Reader Service is committed to protecting your privacy. Our Privacy Policy is available online at www.ReaderService.com or upon request from the Reader Service.
We make a portion of our mailing list available to reputable third parties that offer products we believe may interest you. If you prefer that we not exchange your name with third parties, or if you wish to clarify or modify your communication preferences, please visit us at www.ReaderService.com/consumerschoice or write to us at Reader Service Preference Service, P.O. Box 9062, Buffalo, NY 14269. Include your complete name and address.

FFBPA12